American Tales

by Michael G. Gaunt
Illustrations by Polly Hobbs

Hewitt Homeschooling Resources
2103 B Street
Washougal, WA 98671-0009

Written by Michael G. Gaunt, M.A.
Illustrations by Polly Hobbs
Staff Editors: Christine Dillon, Elisabeth Doucey,
    Donna Fisher, April Purtell, Maria Stein, and
    Gladys Whitted
Special Homeschooler Editorial Staff:
    Nathan Haugaard (Age 8) and Malerie Paynter (Age 8)

Mailing Address . . . .P. O. Box 9, Washougal, WA 98671-0009
Phone . . . .(360) 835-8708
For a free catalog . . .(800) 348-1750
FAX . . . .(360) 835-8697
EMail . . . . .info@hewitthomeschooling.com

Published July 1996
02 01 00 99 98 97 96   7 6 5 4 3 2 1
Printed in the United States of America

Table of Contents

Dear Student,

 Even before we ever take a class in the history of the United States or read a book on the subject, we all hear stories about American heroes. We are told many of these stories over and over again. For example, how many times have you heard the story of George Washington and the cherry tree?

 It is important that we know about American history, but hearing the same old stories many times is sometimes not very fun. That is the problem many people have with history. They have gotten bored with it.

 While I was writing this book, I thought about this. It was because I wanted to make this book interesting that I chose the characters and the stories that I did. You will have heard of many of the people whose stories are told here. Some of the stories will even be ones that you know already. But I hope that most of the stories are new to you. I have also included some people whose stories are almost never told, but who are important and interesting all the same.

 I love history and I want other people to love it, too. That's why I wrote this book. I hope it will help you learn to love history as much as I do.

 Michael Gaunt
 c/o Hewitt Homeschooling Resources
 P.O. Box 9
 Washougal, WA 98671

Dear Student,

My first step in illustrating is careful reading of the story to get to know the characters and the situation.

Step two is deciding which event in the story would best help the reader remember important information. Many pencil sketches, called "roughs," are made and studied to see if they tell an accurate story and are interesting.

Step three is research at the library for correct historical information and details as to clothing, hair styles, footwear, houses, furniture, light sources, writing implements, wagons, harnesses, and horses.

Corrected drawings are made based on the research, then the drawings are transferred to special paper and are painted using transparent watercolor.

I try to do illustrations that make you curious about the story and the people. If you have any comments or questions, I would like to hear from you. Letters may be sent to the following address:

Polly (Poho) Hobbs
c/o Hewitt Homeschooling Resources
P.O. Box 9
Washougal, WA 98671

Introduction

*"If history records good things of good people,
the thoughtful reader is encouraged to imitate
the good; if it records the bad ends of evil people,
the careful listener or reader is encouraged
to avoid doing evil."—Bede*

Feel the Stories

Many of our loves and hates are founded in
childhood. If our exposure is pleasant, we are
likely to develop a *taste* for the food, subject, or
person. And we remember best what involves our
emotions, not just our intellect. This reader was
written with such a goal in mind. Help your
student to feel the wind in the sails with
Columbus, hear the crates of tea slap the water
with Sam Adams, smell the peanuts as George
Carver grinds them, and weep as Robert E. Lee
surrenders to General Grant.

Develop the Skills

These stories are also designed to whet your
student's appetite for more. The stories appear in
chronological order based on the events of the
stories, rather than the birth dates of the featured
person. Your child may want to keep a timeline
as he works through the book. He should have a
sense of the growth of our nation from colony to
frontier to war to birthplace of many scientific
discoveries.

Reading each story may involve several steps,
some of which may require your help. Depending
on your student's ability, encourage him to

1. Locate the place on a map or globe where
the events of the story occurred.

2. Look at the picture. What can be learned from it?

3. Read the story silently.   The vocabulary and structure are consistent between a third- and fourth-grade reading level, so that a child may *successfully* read on his own.

4. Practice narration. Retell the story to you in his own words. Encourage thoroughness.

5. Read aloud (perhaps to a younger sibling). Work on pronunciation, expression, smooth-ness, appropriate volume, speed, rhythm, and intonation. Develop reading poise.

6. List new vocabulary words and check their definitions in a dictionary. Use in a new sentence. Think up synonyms.

7. Answer the content questions marked ❏ in the think box at the end of each story. Discuss the *think-about-it* question marked ○ which occurs at the end of the think box.

8. Generate questions for discussion (prompted by you). Questions that should spring to mind include *What else happened to this person? Why did he decide to do what he did? Did he make good decisions? What was the outcome?* Use resource books to answer questions when answers are not found in the reader.

9. Understand that while all of the historical stories are true, the stories about Billy and Mary are not. Your student may find their behavior a little antagonistic. As in real life, the conflict leads to a principle or moral in the story. Use their behavior to elicit responses from the student as to *how* they *should* have behaved.

10. Look at the picture again. Pick out details that *show* the story. Did he notice the teapot in

the picture of Samuel Adams or the nine Supreme Court Justices in the picture of James Madison?

11. Find and read other age-appropriate books about the people and events for further study.

12. Relate to you what lessons he may have learned from the story that he can apply to his own life experience now or in the future.

Expand the Memory

Use the stories as springboards for other projects. The following are suggested activities for each story, but the only limit is you and your student's imagination: Make a model of one of Columbus' ships, a relief map of papier-mâché of Custer's last battle, role play Jackson standing up to the British, or gaze at the stars and name the constellations as Maria Mitchell did.

Here are some additional ideas your student may use to expand the stories:

✔ State lesson, moral, or point of each story. (comprehension)
✔ If possible, parallel moral with Bible verses.
✔ Remark how moral can apply to his life.
✔ Make murals or dioramas.
✔ Conduct discussions about traits and motivations of the characters in each story.
✔ Research the historical figure from the story. Make an oral presentation or pantomime to the family or write a fictional story or play about an event in the character's life.
✔ Underline suffixes in red and prefixes in green. Break the word into written syllables.
✔ Anticipate what will happen next in a story.

But most of all, enjoy the stories together!

American
Tales

Christopher Columbus
Admiral of the Ocean Sea

Billy, the bold explorer, stumbled out of the forest. There, across the wide, flat plain, he could just make out his base camp. He was almost home. He had made it!

He started out across the plain, keeping an eye out for lions. The sun beat down on him. It was hot. He took off his pith helmet, standard headgear for explorers, and wiped his sweaty face on his sleeve. Not much farther to go now.

At last, he approached the camp. Strangely, no one seemed to be paying attention to him. They kept talking to each other and sipping their lemonade. He wiped his face again and said, "Whew!" very loudly.

His grandfather turned to look at him. "Dr. William, I presume?"

This wasn't really deepest, darkest Africa. Billy and his family were visiting his grandparents' farmhouse in the country. The hat wasn't even Billy's. Grandpa used it for gardening.

"I've discovered that forest," Billy said, pointing back at the woods behind his grandparents' house.

"How could you have discovered it?" his father asked. "We knew it was there all along."

"Well, I just explored it, anyway."

"Did you find anything?" Grandma Elizabeth asked.

"I came up to the back of another farmhouse. I didn't see any people so I claimed the whole area for you," said Billy proudly.

"Well, aren't you just another Christopher Columbus?" Grandpa asked.

"He discovered America, didn't he?"

"Well, not exactly," his grandfather answered. "He couldn't really discover it because there were already people living here when he arrived. They knew it was here. What he did do was explore parts of what are now called the continents of America. He also proved to many people back in Europe that America was here."

"Will you tell me the story?"

"Well, of course I will. I was hoping you would ask me." Grandpa smiled and winked at Billy.

Before Columbus made his voyage, many people in Europe thought the earth was flat like a plate. They thought all of the land was clumped together in the center. This land was called the known world. It included Europe, Africa, and Asia and was surrounded by a body of water called the Ocean Sea. People weren't sure about the shape of the Ocean Sea. Some thought it went on and on forever. Others thought that it ended somewhere and if they sailed too far, they would fall off the edge of the world—just like a pea rolling off a plate.

Grandpa George winked at Billy again. Billy didn't like peas. One way he tried to get rid of them was to roll them off his plate and onto the floor. This didn't usually work. There were always more peas in the bowl to take the place of the ones that rolled away. Grandpa said, "Getting back to the story . . ."

It took a brave person to go against what so many people thought, especially in

3

something like this. If everybody else was right and Columbus was wrong, he would surely die.

As it happened, Columbus was only half right. He was right in thinking that the Earth is a sphere. He thought that if he sailed west from Europe he would reach Asia. The people of Europe were very interested in getting things from Asia like spices and silk. Before Columbus made his voyage, people sailed east around the southern tip of Africa to get to Asia. This was a very long trip. If Columbus could find a quicker way to get to Asia and back, he would become rich selling those things in Europe. But he thought he would only have to cross one ocean if he sailed west from Europe to Asia. In fact, there are two oceans and two large continents between Europe and Asia. When Columbus finally reached land, he thought he was near China or India. Instead he had landed on an island off the American coast.

But I'm getting ahead of my story. Before Columbus could sail anywhere, he had to convince someone to trust him. Isabella, the queen of Spain, finally agreed to loan him three ships: the Niña, the Pinta, and the Santa Maria. In August of 1492, he set sail from Spain. Columbus thought it would only take him a month to sail from Europe to Asia.

After thirty days at sea, the crew began to grumble. "Our captain has been wrong all along. I never liked his plan," they said to each other. "We're going to fall off the edge of the world, I'm sure. We must make Columbus turn around and go back to Spain."

(Billy giggled at Grandpa's Spanish accent.)

Columbus was worried too, but he didn't let the crew know about that. Instead he prayed to God for help. He talked the crew into sailing for just three more days. "If we don't see land by then, we'll turn back. I promise," he said.

They sailed on for two more days. Still, they had not seen any sign of land. Finally on the third day, the crew spotted a flock of birds. They were land birds. The sailors knew they couldn't be far from land now. They steered the boat to follow the birds. The next day, the call came down from the crow's nest. "Tierra! Land!"

That's how close Columbus came to turning around and not finding America. He named the first place they landed San Salvador. The name means Holy Saviour. It was Columbus's way of thanking God for the help he had received in reaching his goal.

When the sailors landed on the island, they were met by a group of natives.

"They don't look Chinese," one of Columbus's men pointed out.

"Perhaps we're near India, instead," said Columbus. He wasn't, of course. He was on an island in the Caribbean south of Florida. But because he thought the natives might be from India, he called them Indians. And that is why all Native Americans are called Indians.

When Columbus arrived back in Europe, he was a hero. Queen Isabella held a huge feast in his honor. She also gave him the title of Admiral of the Ocean Sea. It's funny to think, though, that what they thought they were celebrating wasn't really true. Everyone thought that he had found a quick way to Asia. He hadn't. Columbus sailed to the Americas three more times. By the end of his travels, some people had begun to think that what Columbus had found was a new world. Of course, it was only new to the people of Europe. It was very old indeed to the Native Americans who were already living there.

"So, Columbus didn't really discover America," Billy said. He was thinking hard about his grandfather's story.

"That's right, Billy," Grandpa George answered.

"But he was the first person from Europe to go there, right? It was up to him to show everybody else that it was here."

"Well, that's not quite true either," Grandpa said.

"If he wasn't the first, then why didn't other people know the Americas were there?" Billy was beginning to get very confused.

"The other people who visited America before Columbus didn't tell their stories to many people. They weren't working for a famous queen like Isabella. In fact, few people even now have heard of them," Grandpa explained.

"Do you know their stories, Grandpa?" Billy wanted to know. Adventure stories were his favorites. He hoped his grandfather could tell him a lot of them.

"I've heard a couple of stories," Grandpa admitted, "but I'm not an expert in telling them. You should ask your mother and your grandmother for those stories. I bet they each have one they could tell you."

Billy looked eagerly at his mother and grandmother. "I'm sure we do have some stories to tell, but not right now," his mother said. "It's almost dinner time. Maybe later one of us can tell you a story about other European explorers in the Americas. Now you go get cleaned up, my little discoverer."

Billy pulled his hat down over his eyes and crawled off through the tall grass toward his home base. He was looking around for lions again. 🌿

❑ Name the three ships Queen Isabella loaned Columbus.

❑ Why are Native Americans called Indians?

❑ When Christopher Columbus was hunting for a new land, how did some people think the earth was shaped?

○ The crew grumbled, complained, and thought they should turn back. When others grumble about what you are trying to do, how do you act? Do you give up or keep trying? What did Columbus say and do?

Leif Erikson
Leif the Lucky

That night Grandma fixed some of Billy's favorite foods. They had fried chicken, mashed potatoes with gravy, and grits with cheese. They also had peas. This time Billy ate all the peas on his plate. Remembering the story his grandfather had told him that afternoon, he imagined he was a sea monster gobbling up sailors.

Despite the good food, he could barely sit still. He couldn't wait for the meal to be over. He wanted to hear the story about the other European explorer of America.

Mary, Billy's sister, hadn't heard the story about Christopher Columbus that afternoon. She had been taking a nap. The hot weather at Grandma's house made her tired, she said. She also hadn't heard the promise to tell a story that evening about another explorer. Billy had told her about it before dinner. Like Billy, she didn't know who it could be. She didn't know any stories about explorers who had come to America before Columbus.

Finally, dinner was over and the dishes were done. Everyone settled down in the living room.

"This is a story my own grandfather used to tell," Grandma Elizabeth began. "He liked to tell stories about the Vikings. The Vikings had many stories they called sagas. Some of them were adventure stories about sailors at sea or explorers of strange lands. Others were about arguments between people. The Vikings loved to sail and they loved to argue. They also loved to tell stories.

"My grandfather was born in Norway. That is a country in the northern part of Europe. It is one of the places where the Vikings lived. My grandfather looked like a Viking. He was tall and blonde, and he had a great big beard. He loved to do Viking things. He had a sailboat, and sometimes he would take us grandchildren out on the lake near his house. He could really argue, too. He would argue with just about anybody except my grandma. And he would tell us stories. This was one of his favorites."

There once was a man named Erik the Red. People called him "Red" because of the color of his hair. He had long flowing hair and a great bushy beard that looked like flame when the sun shone on them. He lived in peace for a while in Iceland. Iceland is an island far to the north. He grew bored with peace, however, and became an outlaw. The court of Iceland, which was called the Allthing, told him he would have to leave the country. He wasn't sad about this order. He had had enough of Iceland. He was ready to go exploring.

Erik had heard stories of a land of ice to the west of Iceland. He went in search of that land. He sailed for six days through uncharted waters. Then, on the seventh morning, he saw mountains of ice rising up through the clouds. He spent three years sailing around this new land. Erik was looking for a pleasant place to set up a village. Ice covered much of the land all year. He began to think there was no place in this new land where he could live. Finally, he found some places which were green and lovely during the summer. He could make a home there.

Erik sneaked back to Iceland. He was still not allowed to go back to his home to stay. He had only returned to gather a few bold people like himself. Erik was looking for people who would not be afraid to leave their homes and begin a new life in the land he had discovered. He had decided to call this new land Greenland. He thought that if the place had a pretty name, more people would want to come back to this new land with him. He did find some people who were interested in this kind of adventure. They brought their families, their farm animals, and their seeds. These were the first farmers in Greenland.

Not long after Erik went back to Greenland with his new friends, another sailor tried to follow them. His name was Bjarni. His boat was blown off course and into thick fog. A few days later, when the fog finally cleared, he began searching for Greenland. Bjarni had been told that Greenland was full of tall, icy mountains and had no trees. It had grassy spaces between the icy mountains and the sea where people could live and farm. He thought he would recognize it when he saw it.

The first land Bjarni saw when he came out of the fog had woods and low hills. It was a beautiful land, but he knew it was not Greenland. Bjarni sailed on.

The next land he saw was completely flat. Forests covered this land. This wasn't Greenland either. Bjarni sailed on.

The third land he saw had icy mountains, but he knew this was not Greenland, either. It didn't have grassy spaces between the mountains and the sea. Instead, large flat stones covered the land. Bjarni sailed on.

The fourth land he saw also had large icy mountains, but here green grass covered the spaces between the mountains and the sea. At last Bjarni had found Greenland. He went to Erik's house and told him what had happened and about the lands he had seen.

The other Vikings in Greenland laughed at Bjarni. They said he hadn't acted much like a Viking. Vikings were supposed to be brave and curious explorers. But Bjarni hadn't explored any of the lands he had seen.

One of the Vikings who laughed at Bjarni was named Leif Erikson. People called him "Erikson" because Erik the Red was his father.

"Does that mean we're called Anderson because we are children of someone named Ander?" Mary asked.

"A long time ago, maybe, that might have happened," Grandma answered. "Or maybe the person's name was Andrew, and the name changed over the years."

"That's neat," Mary said. "Our name really means something."

"What did Leif Erikson do?" Billy wanted to know. He was anxious to get back to the story.

Leif wanted to explore the lands that Bjarni had seen. He bought Bjarni's boat. Leif thought that since the boat had been to those lands before, it would know the way and would be able to take him there. Then, he set sail with a group of about thirty other Vikings. He saw each of the lands Bjarni had seen. But he saw them in the opposite order.

The first land Leif Erikson saw was the land of icy mountains and flat stones. He called it Helluland. That meant "Flat Stone Land" in his language. We now call it Baffin Island.

The next land he reached was flat and wooded. He called it Markland. That meant "Wood Land" in his language. We now call it Labrador.

Finally, he came to the land with forests and rolling hills. This was the prettiest land of all but he didn't know what to call it. He landed his boat, and all of his men went ashore to explore.

Not long after they landed, the sailors found wide fields of wheat. They also found hills covered with grapevines. Now Erik knew what he could call this land. He named it

Vinland the Good. Vinland meant "Vine Land." Vinland was probably what we now call Newfoundland or New England. Leif Erikson became known as Leif the Lucky because he had found such a beautiful land.

Soon other Vikings visited. They liked it so much they stayed. They built some houses near the coast. Not long after that, some natives came to the Viking village in Vinland. They wanted to trade furs for weapons. When the Vikings wouldn't give them anything but milk for their furs, the natives attacked.

The Vikings decided this new land was too dangerous. The Vikings were brave, but there were too many natives in Vinland and not enough Vikings to protect themselves. As soon as they could, they left Vinland and went back to Greenland. After that, the only reason Vikings went to Vinland was to gather grapes, wheat, and wood. They didn't stay long enough to be bothered by the natives.

"All these things happened almost 500 years before Columbus sailed to America," Grandma said. "That is the same amount of time it has been since Columbus visited until now."

"Why don't we have a Leif Erikson day instead of Columbus Day?" Billy asked.

"My grandfather used to ask the same question after he came to this country. One reason is that few people know what Leif did. Another reason is that Leif's explorations didn't have a big effect on Europe. Not many people tried to find Vinland the Good after Leif went there. The same thing is not true of Christopher Columbus's voyages. Many people were interested in what he had done. He caused quite a stir."

Mary asked, "Did other explorers come to America?"

"Yes, they did," her mother answered, "but those stories will have to wait for another day."

With sad faces and some complaining, Billy and Mary went off to bed. They both dreamed about discovering new worlds. ✼

[Sometimes the spelling of the names of historical figures is changed to make them more familiar. This has happened with Leif Erikson's name. Since Eric is usually spelled with a *c* now, Leif's name is often spelled "Ericson." That is the way it can usually be found in dictionaries and encyclopedias. It is sometimes found under "Leif." I have chosen to spell his name with a *k* because it is closer to the way the Vikings would have spelled it. Leif himself probably spelled his name "Eiriksson."]

❑ What is a saga?

❑ The story talks about Erik sailing in "uncharted" waters. What does that mean?

❑ In the story you discovered how some people got their names. Why was Erik called Erik the Red? How did Leif Erikson get his last name? Do you know some unusual names? How did your parents choose your name? Do you have a nickname?

○ What character traits that Leif Erikson had would you like to develop? How will they help you?

Pocahontas
The Brave Little Girl

Billy, Tommy, and most of the kids from the neighborhood came running around the corner of the house. They were whooping and hollering and making an awful racket. It was hard to tell that half of this crowd was chasing the other half. They ran into Tommy's yard next door where a kind of camp had been built. Mary couldn't tell whether it was the Indians' camp or the soldiers' fort.

Mary was sitting on her front steps. Her chin was resting on her hands, and her elbows on her knees. She had frowned at the other children as they ran by, but she didn't get up to play with them. She kept frowning after they had gone by.

Just as one group of children had broken into the camp or fort, Mary's mother came out on the porch. She was carrying a cup of coffee and a magazine. She saw Mary and sat down on the steps beside her. "Are they not letting you play?"

"No, it's not that," Mary replied. "I didn't want to play."

"Why not, dear?"

"I've been thinking," Mary answered.

"That must be why you have those frown lines on your forehead." Her mother rubbed Mary's forehead with her thumb trying to rub away the lines. Mary giggled as she tried to dodge out of the way.

"Okay, then tell me, Mary," her mother continued, "what have you been thinking about that has kept you from playing with everyone else?"

"I was thinking about the cowboys-and-Indians game. That's what they're playing."

"I couldn't tell what they were doing except making a lot of noise."

"It's cowboys and Indians," said Mary. "The Indians always try to get the cowboys, and the cowboys always try to get the Indians. I guess that's because that's what the real cowboys and Indians were like. But weren't they ever friends? Were they always trying to get each other?"

"Well, it was hard for the cowboys and settlers to get along with the Indians," answered Mary's mother. · "This was because they all wanted the same thing. The cowboys and settlers wanted the Indians' land. Of course, the Indians wanted to keep their own lands. I do know a story about a settler and a little Indian girl who become friends. The Indian girl was just about your age. Would you like to hear the story?"

"Oh, yes, please." Mary's face brightened.

This is the story of Pocahontas. Pocahontas was a lively little Indian girl. Her name meant "playful one." She was a beautiful girl, and she was her father's favorite child. Pocahontas' father was called Powhatan. He was a chief of the Algonquin Indians. They lived in what we now call Virginia.

In 1607, Captain John Smith led a group of settlers to a place in Powhatan's land. The settlers had come all the way across the Atlantic Ocean from England to settle there. They called their settlement Jamestown after their king, James the First, of England. This was long before there was anything called the United States. America was a wilderness and only American Indians lived here.

Chief Powhatan did not want to give any of his land to the English settlers. Other members of his tribe tried to change his mind. "Oh, great chief," they said, "think of the treasures we might be able to get from these newcomers. They have great power. See the giant sailing boat they use? Perhaps we can trade with them. If we give them some of what we have, maybe they will give us some great treasures from far away."

Powhatan agreed to let the Englishmen build their town. He was curious about what these new people might want to give the Indians. But still, neither group really trusted the other.

"See? That's just what I mean," Mary interrupted. "Even right from the beginning, the Indians and settlers didn't like each other."

"It's true that there were some Indians and some settlers who didn't trust each other, Mary. But I haven't gotten to Pocahontas' part of the story. Wait and see what she does."

Just a few months after the settlers arrived, something very important happened. This was something that would change the way the Indians and the settlers felt about each other. One day while Captain Smith was away from Jamestown trading with the Indians, he was captured. He didn't know what was going on. He was taken to see Chief Powhatan.

When John Smith arrived at Powhatan's village he was led into a large building. Many members of the Algonquin tribe were already inside. Powhatan sat at the far end of the building. He was surrounded by his family, including Pocahontas. John Smith sat on the ground in front of the chief. As soon as Smith sat down, the Indians started discussing what they should do with him.

Some said, "We must kill this man. Then the rest of the settlers will be scared, and they will go away. Why should we give them any of our land?"

Others said, "Look at all of the things we have gotten from these men. A little land is a small price to pay for all of these treasures."

In the end, Powhatan was sorry he had given away any of his land. He was willing to do what some of his people suggested. He was willing to kill John Smith to drive the other settlers away. Just as the Indians were about to kill the Captain, Pocahontas ran forward. She was only ten or eleven years old, but she was very brave. She stepped in front of John Smith to shield him from the other Indians.

What Pocahontas did was an important thing. By saving John Smith's life, she had brought him into the Algonquin Tribe. She now thought of John as her brother. Powhatan thought of Captain Smith as his own son. The anger the Indians had felt against the settlers was forgotten very quickly. Now there would be nothing but friendship between the two groups . . . .

Well, that was the way it was supposed to be. From then on John Smith certainly got along well with the Indians, especially his new little sister, Pocahontas. She often came into Jamestown to visit with John. They would play together or just talk. Sometimes they would trade small things like pieces of cloth or glass beads, but not all of the settlers were happy to be closer to the Indians.

Getting a settlement started is hard work. Things did not always go well for the Jamestown Colony. The settlers blamed John Smith for their problems since he was the leader. It didn't take long for the settlers to dislike Smith and everything he did. That included being friends with Indians. In 1610, only three years after they had arrived in Virginia, the settlers forced John Smith to sail back to England. Another man replaced him as leader of Jamestown.

Pocahontas was heartbroken. Her big brother had left. None of the other settlers were ready to make friends with the Indians.

In England, many people heard the story of Pocahontas. John Smith told it many times. People were amazed at the bravery and generosity of the little Indian girl. They were surprised that she had been willing to invite a European to join her tribe.

It didn't take long for Pocahontas to become famous. She was so well known that people thought she should be brought to England to meet the king. Pocahontas enchanted James the First and the entire royal court. She was happy to meet the king and to be able to see her friend, John Smith, again. Unfortunately, she was not used to the cold, wet weather that is common in England. She was from Virginia, remember. She became very ill and died on the boat on her way back home. But Pocahontas was not forgotten. Everywhere the story was told of the brave little Indian girl who had tried to show that Indians and settlers could live together.

"So you see, dear," Mary's mother said, "it is possible for Indians and settlers to be friends."

"But not very often, I guess," Mary said.

"No, not very often," said her mother sadly.

"Okay. Thanks," Mary said. "I'm going to go play now."

"You're going to play cowboys and Indians?"

"Yes. I'm going to be Pocahontas. I'm going to go make friends." Mary jumped off the steps and ran over to where the children were playing in the next yard. Her mother smiled after her. ❧

Katherine Anderson's Think Box

❏ The Indians did not want to give any of their land to the white men who had come from England. What did some of the Indians want to do with John Smith?

❏ What did Pocahontas do to help John Smith?

○ Even children can do important things to help people. What can you do to help your family, friends, and others? What does Jesus say about being kind to others?

Benjamin Franklin

Founder of the Junto Club

"Can you help me in the garage, Aunt Anne?" Mary asked. Aunt Anne and Uncle Bob were visiting for the weekend.

"Are you working on the car again, dear?' her aunt asked.

"No," Mary laughed. "I need some help with the refrigerator box."

"I don't think you should be moving heavy pieces of furniture," said Aunt Anne.

"I'm not doing that either," laughed Mary again. "The box is empty. I'm using it as a clubhouse."

"That's a good idea," her aunt said. "Why didn't you say that in the first place instead of trying to confuse your old aunt?"

Mary giggled. She took her aunt's hand and pulled her toward the garage. "Do you want to be in my club?" she asked.

"I'd love to, dear," Aunt Anne responded, "but do you really want an old person like me in your club?"

"Sure," said Mary. "How old you are doesn't matter. To be in this club, you only have to be a girl."

Now Aunt Anne laughed. "I guess I could pass for a girl. Are you sure you don't want your brother in your club?"

"He has his own new club," Mary explained. "It's only for boys."

"I see. What are you going to do in your club?"

Mary shook her head. "I don't know yet. I want it to be a new kind of club. I want it to be better than Billy's."

The refrigerator box was in one corner of the garage. There were other empty boxes in front of it. When Mary and Aunt Anne had moved those out of the way, they found more empty boxes inside the refrigerator box. They finally got all of the extra boxes stacked up again in the corner. They laid the refrigerator box down on its side so Mary could crawl in and out of it.

"Can I still be in your club if I don't climb into the clubhouse?" asked Aunt Anne.

"Okay," answered Mary.

"Now you should decide what you are going to do in your club," her aunt said. "What do you like to do?"

"I don't know," said Mary.

"Well, you like to play, don't you? You like to ride your bike."

"Yes, I like those things," answered Mary, "but so does Billy. That's what he's going to do in his club. I wanted mine to be different. Mine has to be better."

Mary's aunt asked, "Do you like to do other things?"

"I like to read," said Mary thoughtfully. "I also like to explore things, but can I have a club about those things?"

"Of course you can. Those things would make a great club. In fact, that kind of club reminds me of one that was started by a famous American. Would you like to hear about it?"

"Yes, please." Mary lay down on her stomach in her clubhouse box.

"This is the story of Benjamin Franklin. I'm sure you've already heard many stories about him. That is because he did so many things. But you probably haven't heard this one."

Benjamin Franklin was the youngest of seventeen brothers and sisters. He was born in 1706 and grew up in Boston. That was a long time before this land became the United States. He was already 70 years old before America won its freedom from England.

When he was growing up, Benjamin wanted to be a sea captain. His parents had other ideas. They wanted him to be a preacher. Things didn't work out either of those ways. Even though he had time to be many things in his long life, he never held either of those two jobs. When he was twelve, he was sent to work with his oldest brother, James. James was a newspaper publisher.

Newspapers were very important at that time. They reported the news just as they do now, but they also did something else. In those days, it was hard to get from one place to another. There weren't any cars. There weren't many paved roads. It was hard for people to get together and talk about important ideas. The newspapers helped this. People could talk to each other through the newspapers. They would write letters to the newspapers, and other people could read them. That's the way people talked about politics or other important ideas.

Newspaper publishers became important people because of the importance of newspapers. The publishers served as the newspapers' editors. That means they chose what to put in their newspapers. They also wrote many of the stories. Newspaper publishers even printed the papers themselves.

Working for the newspaper was a great job for Benjamin Franklin. He had many good ideas about politics and other important things. He learned how to write well so that other people wanted to read about his ideas.

But he had a problem at first. Because he was working for his brother, it was hard for him to get his stories published. Sometimes brothers and sisters don't see each other in the same way that other people see them.

"Maybe you know what I mean," Aunt Anne said. "What do you think about Billy's ideas?"

"That's different. He really does come up with lots of bad ideas, except for having a club. That was his idea, I guess."

Anyway, James didn't think Benjamin was very smart. He wouldn't publish stories that Benjamin had written. Benjamin had to trick his brother in order to get his stories into the paper. He sent his stories to James without signing them. As long as James didn't know that Benjamin had written them, he was able to see how good they were.

When he was sixteen, Benjamin Franklin moved to Philadelphia. He wanted to work on a paper where it would be easier to publish his stories. He did very well there. Not many years later, he was able to publish his own newspaper. He became an important person in Philadelphia. Many people read what he thought about the events that were going on at that time.

While he was in Philadelphia, he started his club. It was called the Junto Club. It was another way for people to be able to come together and talk about their ideas. Each club meeting started with the same questions. Here are some of them:

Have you read anything which you think other members of the club would like to read?

Do you know of anyone who has done something good recently?

Do you know of anyone whom the members of this club should help?

Do you know of any important things which we should talk about?

Do you know of anything which we should try to change or make better?

Is there some way that the members of this club can help you?

Is there something you think the members of this club can do?

What good things has someone done for you recently?

These and other questions were asked each time Benjamin's Junto Club met. It was partly because of this club that Benjamin helped set up the first lending library. That way more people could read the books that other people liked.

The club also sparked Benjamin's interest in scientific experiments. You've probably heard about some of the things he did. He experimented with electricity by flying a kite in a thunder storm. That was a dangerous experiment. Benjamin also invented a better wood stove and bifocal glasses. Bifocals let people with poor eyesight see things that are close and other things that are far away. He also did many things to help Philadelphia. He set up a fire department. He arranged to have the streets of the city paved and lighted. His club came up with many helpful and useful ideas.

"Do you think if I had a club like that we could do some of those same things?" asked Mary.

"Well," said Aunt Anne, "we already have a fire department and street lights. But your club could come up with new ways to be helpful. Your club could also do other things that Benjamin Franklin did. You could start a newspaper."

"Wow! That sounds like a great club. You'll help us with that stuff, won't you?"

"Of course, dear," said her aunt. "That's what it means to be in a club. Everybody helps everybody else."

"This is going to be a much better club than Billy's," Mary grinned.

Mary went to get her magic markers. She wrote "Mary's Junto Club" in big letters on the side of the refrigerator box. Aunt Anne helped her to spell "Junto." Then they settled down to begin their first meeting.

"Have you read anything that you think I would like to read?" asked Aunt Anne. 🌿

Aunt Anne Anderson's Think Box

❏ When Benjamin was only twelve where did his parents send him to work?

❏ Why were newspapers so important at that time? Why didn't people listen to the radio or television?

❏ Benjamin had good ideas and wrote good stories. What other important things did he do?

○ What kind of club would you like to start? Think about useful things you can do or make to help others. What would you like to invent?

Daniel Boone

The Daring Frontiersman

"Why do Grandma and Grandpa Williams live so far away?" asked Billy. He was watching his father put their suitcases into the trunk of the car. Billy's family was about to leave on a trip. It was going to be a long one. His father said it would take two whole days just to drive to Grandma and Grandpa's house. "Why don't Mom's parents live nearby like yours?"

"Your grandparents found a place that they liked and decided to live there," his father explained. "Your mother and I found a different place where we wanted to live."

"But they're so far away," Billy complained. He was not looking forward to a long trip in the car. He was sure he was going to be bored.

"Well, I guess that's everything." Billy's father closed the trunk. "Let's go inside and make sure your mother is packing enough sandwiches for lunch. Driving always makes me extra hungry."

"Okay." As they walked back to the house, Billy hung his head and dragged his feet.

"I know you think you can't have fun in a car for two days," Billy's father said, "but you may be surprised. There are many interesting things to see along the way."

"But it's still a long way." Billy had made up his mind not to enjoy this trip no matter what his father said.

Dad said, "You're right. It is a long way. One of the reasons we live so far apart is that this country is so big. That's because a lot of brave men and women kept moving farther and farther away from their homes. They claimed new land for the United States and then moved again farther into the wilderness. If you like, I will tell you the story of one of those brave people. It might help pass some of the traveling time."

"That would be okay, I guess." Billy had decided that there would be nothing good about this trip. If his father told a good story, maybe he would change his mind.

Pretty soon, the whole family was in the car and driving away. Billy and his sister, Mary, waved good-bye to their house. She had the same idea as Billy. Two days in the car was a long time.

As they drove down the street, they passed the houses of many of Billy's friends. He waved good-bye to those houses as he had waved to his own. They turned onto a larger street. They passed the grocery store where Billy helped his Mom shop. They went by the movie theater and the restaurant where they had celebrated Billy's last birthday. Then Billy didn't recognize any more stores. Everything he knew was behind him now. He didn't know what he was going to see next. It would be like that for the next two days in the car.

Billy thought about what his father had said before they left. Brave men and women had left their homes to see new things. Billy decided he wanted to be one of those brave men. He wanted to see new things. "Dad," he said, "will you tell me that story now? Will you tell me about the people who left their homes to go into the wilderness?"

"Sure," said his father. "I'll tell you the story of Daniel Boone."

Daniel Boone was born in 1734 before there was a country called the United States. At that time, it was just a group of small colonies. Most people from England lived near the East Coast. Few people had gone into the western part of this land. Much of the West was still controlled by the Indians.

It was not a surprise that Daniel Boone became a pioneer. It seemed that his whole family wanted to live far away from most other folks. When Daniel was still a young man, his family moved from Pennsylvania to a remote part of North Carolina. The Boone family had not been in North Carolina long when Daniel started dreaming about places even more wild.

There were only a few English settlers who had been west of North Carolina. They were mostly traders or hunters. These people made deals with the Indians to hunt on Indian land. In return, they gave the Indians things such as hatchets and cloth.

Daniel Boone spoke to every trader he met. He became good friends with one of them, a man named John Finley.

"You must see Kentucky, Daniel," Finley told him. "It's just across the Cumberland Mountains from North Carolina. Kentucky is a great place for hunting. It's full of deer and lots of other animals. Nobody lives there but Indians. You can easily be hundreds of miles from any other European."

"That sounds great." Daniel said. "I love to go hunting in the woods without a lot of other folks cluttering up the place."

"And there's more," Finley went on. "The land there is very rich. It would be a great place for a young man with a family to set up a farm. I'll bet you couldn't stop the corn from growing in a place like that even if you wanted to."

Daniel Boone enjoyed his talks with John Finley very much. When Finley moved on, Daniel dreamed about farming and hunting in the new land. He didn't get a chance to fulfill those dreams until many years later.

Daniel married and had children of his own, but he stayed on the family farm. After a while, the Boone farm began to fail. Crops became smaller, and the Boone family was unable to make enough money to support everyone. Daniel decided that it was time to move his family. He wanted to set up a new farm in the rich land of Kentucky. He wondered how he could do it.

About that time, his friend John Finley visited him. "Come with me on a hunting trip to Kentucky," Finley said. "I'm just about to go there with a few other men. They are looking for new places to live, too. While we're hunting, you can look for a good place for your new farm."

"That's a great idea." said Daniel. "You can show me all of the best places you know. My family can use the extra money I'll make from selling the skins of the deer we'll hunt."

The Indians of Kentucky didn't like hunters coming onto their land. The hunters killed deer that the Indians wanted to use themselves. On this trip, the Indians captured Daniel Boone and one other member of his group. The Indians warned them never to come back to Kentucky. After the warning, the two hunters were allowed to go back to North Carolina.

But Daniel was determined. Even though he had been warned, he went back to Kentucky a few months later. He was still looking for a place where his family could live.

One day while hunting in Kentucky, Daniel was walking along the edge of a cliff. A long way below him a river ran through the canyon. Suddenly, up ahead, he saw a group of Indians. When he turned around to go back the other way, he saw another group of Indians who had been following him. Then, he saw there was another group coming at him from the side. The Indians had warned him not to come back, and here he was. He didn't know what they would do to him this time. The river was too far below him for him to jump into it. There was a very tall tree growing up from the riverbank. The top of the tree was right next to the place where Daniel was trapped. To escape the Indians, he did the only thing he could. Daniel jumped from the cliff into the tree and then climbed down to the river. None of the Indians were brave enough to follow him.

His dream of finding a new home finally came true in 1775. That was five years after his first trip. That year, he made a permanent home in Kentucky. He led a large group of settlers there, and they set up a town called Boonesborough.

The Indians hadn't liked it when the hunters came one by one. You can imagine how they felt about a whole town on their lands. They attacked Boonesborough often. The settlers stayed safe only because they built a high wall, or stockade, around their town. The Indians couldn't get through it. Boonesborough survived and became an important town.

Over the years, other settlers followed Daniel Boone into Kentucky. Other villages and towns were set up. For a long time, the new settlers had to fight against the Indians. All of the new settlers looked up to Daniel because he had started the first town. He was elected to several public offices.

After a while, Kentucky became too crowded for him, so he decided to move even farther west. Daniel liked to live where there weren't many settlers. He moved to Missouri and lived there for the last twenty years of his life. When he was 85, he was still making long hunting trips even farther to the west. For his whole life, he was never as happy as when he was in the wildest country he could find.

"So is that why you don't live where our grandparents live?" asked Mary. "Are you looking for wilder country?" Everybody laughed.

"And where is Andersonsborough, Dad?" Billy asked. "You moved west, but you didn't set up your own town."

"I'm afraid it doesn't work like that anymore," their father answered. "The country is too full of people now. When I got where I wanted to live, there was already a town there. I didn't need to start my own. You kids probably won't have a town named after you, either."

"The best thing about your story, dear," Mom said, "is that it's already lunch time."

"Are we there yet?" asked Mary.

"Not quite," Dad said.

"I hope you know some more stories," said Billy. "A lot more stories." ❦

❑ Daniel Boone wanted to find better land for farming and hunting. What did he decide to do?

❑ What was the name given to the new settlement in Kentucky named after Daniel Boone?

❑ Did Daniel have a family? In what ways might his wife and children have needed to be brave?

○ In what ways can you be brave now? How will this help you in the future?

Samuel Adams
Son of Liberty

"Please," begged Mary as she followed Billy into the living room.

"No," shouted Billy. "Never!" He sat down on the couch next to his Grandma Elizabeth.

"Now what are you two fighting about?" she asked.

"He won't play with me," Mary complained.

"She wants to have a stupid tea party. That's a girl's game. I'm not going to be in any tea party," Billy said firmly.

"I know a tea party you would have liked to attend," Grandma said.

"There aren't any I would have wanted to be at." Billy was sure.

"This was a very special one. If you two will sit up here quietly and be good, I'll tell you the story," she said.

The children were both interested now. What kind of special tea party could Grandma mean? They both nestled up close to their grandmother, one under each arm, so they could listen.

The party I am talking about happened a long time ago. It was such a long time ago that there wasn't yet a United States. Each of the states was called a colony of England because England still controlled our government.

This tea party happened in Boston. Boston is a city in Massachusetts on the east coast of our country. It wasn't really a tea party; it was just called that. It was actually a protest against England. Many people wanted independence from England. They wanted to be able to run their own government.

In May of the year 1773, the English government started to tax tea. That meant that every time someone in the colonies bought tea he would have to pay a little extra money. This extra money went to George the Third who was the king of England.

Boston was a town full of coffee houses and meeting places. The people were interested in politics. Everywhere people were talking about the new tax. "Why should we pay to support the king?" they asked each other. "If we're going to pay taxes, they should be used for our benefit."

Boston also had several newspapers. Many of these papers were full of complaints about the new tax. "Why should we accept a tax that we haven't had a chance to vote on?" the papers asked. "Taxation without representation is unfair. It is tyranny!" Tyranny happens when the people are not allowed to decide how they will be governed. The king of England was a tyrant because he ruled the colonies without letting them make any decisions for themselves.

Although many people all over the colonies were angry about the tea tax, not everyone was. Most people, whether they wanted independence from England or not, thought of themselves as English. Those people who were most attached to the mother country were willing to pay the tax. "If our king decrees a tax, I shall pay it. It is his God-given right to decide how I shall live. I would no sooner go against my king than I would turn my back on God. Besides, the tax is a small amount. It is only about three pennies for every pound of tea."

"The amount of the tax is not what is important," Samuel Adams declared. Sam Adams lived in Boston. He was a cousin of our second president, John Adams. Sam was one of the people who most wanted independence from England. "What is important is the tax itself. If we pay the tax, that will mean that we agree that the English king has the right to tax us. I say he does not have that right. We are an independent nation. We must live independently. We must govern ourselves."

These were strong words, but many people agreed with him.

The English had chosen to tax tea because tea was so popular. Almost everyone drank tea. It was an English tradition. In the afternoon, people would often have a small meal of sandwiches or cake served with tea. Those people who agreed that the tea tax was a bad thing promised to stop drinking tea. Women no longer gave tea parties. Now they had "no-tea" parties.

"That's the only kind of tea party I would go to," Billy interrupted. "A no-tea party sounds just fine."

Mary glared at Billy, but Grandma pretended to ignore him. She went on with her story.

Late in the fall of 1773, three ships arrived in Boston Harbor. They had come from England. Each carried a large amount of tea which some of the newspapers were calling "that hated weed." Sam Adams and his friends held many meetings to decide what to do about the ships and their cargo.

"We cannot allow those ships to be unloaded," Adams said. "If the tea reaches the shore, the tax will have to be paid. If the tax is paid, all of our efforts will have been for nothing. England and George the Third will think they have the right to tax us."

"But what can we do?" his friends asked.

"We must try to convince the governor to send the ships back to England," Sam answered. "If that doesn't work, we will have no choice but to destroy the tea."

The governor's name was Thomas Hutchinson. He had been chosen by George the Third. It seemed quite unlikely that he would go against the wishes of the king. In fact, he did not. He refused to send the ships back to England. Instead, he demanded that they be unloaded. The governor did not know how serious the tea tax was to Samuel Adams, his friends, and most of the people of Boston. He thought that if he was firm the people would obey. He was wrong.

On the night of December 16, 1773, one last public meeting was held. The people sent a messenger to the governor. "Will you send the ships back to England still loaded with the tea?" the messenger asked.

"I will not," answered Hutchinson. "Those boats must be unloaded."

When the messenger brought this reply back to the meeting, everyone was angry. Samuel Adams rose to his feet and gave the secret sign that their other plan would now be carried out. He said, "This meeting can do nothing more to save the country." When his friends heard this, they knew what to do.

Many of Sam's friends were in a group called the Sons of Liberty. They disguised themselves as Mohawk Indians by wearing feathers and rubbing red brick dust or charcoal on their faces. They did not think anyone would really believe they were Indians. They just did it so they wouldn't be recognized and arrested. The fake Indians boarded the boats and threw the tea into the water. Later they boasted, "We made Boston Harbor into a giant tea cup for King George to drink from."

The tax was not paid; and soon after that, the colonies were at war with England. The result of that war was that we became the United States of America. We got our independence. The war is called the American Revolution, and the night the tea was dumped into the harbor is called the Boston Tea Party.

"You're right, Grandma," Billy said. "That's the only kind of tea party I'm interested in. Do you want to throw all of your tea into the water?" he asked Mary.

"Of course not," Mary said.

"Then I'm going outside," said Billy and he ran out of the room.

Mary looked sad. "That's all right, dear," Grandma Elizabeth said. "You and I can have our own tea party."

Mary smiled at her grandmother and took her hand. She led her upstairs where the tea things were already set for a party. ❧

❏ When Samuel Adams and his friends thought the tea tax was unfair, what did they decide to do about it first? When that did not work, what was their second plan?

❏ Who were the Sons of Liberty? Why did they dress up like Indians? Did they make the right choice when they made the "giant tea cup for King George?"

○ After Grandmother told the story of Samuel Adams and the famous "tea party" did Billy want to have a tea party with Mary? Think of ways he could have been more polite and courteous to his sister even if he didn't want to play.

Andrew Jackson

The Boy Hero

"I got another one! I got another one!
See?" Mary opened her hands to show
Billy the little bug. They both watched it fly
away. "That's four catches each. We're even."

Billy and Mary were chasing fireflies around
the front yard. In the past, they had tried

keeping the bugs in glass jars, punching holes in the lids so the fireflies had air to breathe. But the insects didn't live long. So now the children just grabbed them, being very careful not to hurt them. Then they would let the bugs fly away. It had become a favorite contest to see which of them could catch the most before bedtime.

Bedtime would be pretty soon now. It was late in May so it was warm all night. It was already dark, and the children knew that in a short time their parents would come out and send them off to bed. Neither would win the game unless one of them could catch another firefly.

They were both concentrating hard on the bugs when their grandfather came out on the porch. They didn't hear him until he called out, "Hey, kids, how would you like to hear a story?" They both squealed in surprise.

Just then Mary caught another firefly. "There, that's five. I win." With that she ran up on the porch. "Tell us a story now, Grandpa."

Billy frowned, a little disappointed that he had lost. He usually won this game.

"What kind of story would you like to hear?" Grandpa George asked.

"I want to hear a story about a brave hero," Billy said. That was his favorite kind of story. He thought that would cheer him up. "Do you know any stories where the hero is a kid like us?"

Grandpa had to think about that for a minute. "Sure I do," he said at last.

This is a story about Andrew Jackson, the seventh president of the United States. He certainly was a hero. He was a hero early in his life.

Andrew was born in 1767, a few years before the American Revolution. When he was a child, the states in America were still colonies of England. He was about your age when the war began. One of the things that made him a hero was how young he was when he fought for independence. America had a hard time winning its freedom. We didn't have a trained army; and worst of all, we were fighting a strong country.

"Do you know what country that was? Who did America have to fight to win its freedom?" Grandpa George asked.

"England, of course," answered Billy.

"That's right." Grandpa patted him on the knee and then continued his story.

So, with such a strong enemy, just about everyone who could fight was allowed to join the American army. This included young Andrew Jackson. He wasn't the only child in the army, but he was one of the proudest and most daring.

"What do you think it would be like to be in the army at your age?" Grandpa asked. "I think it would be pretty awful," he said, answering his own question before either Mary or Billy had a chance. "Always cold and wet and tired. There would be no good food and no time to play. Andrew seemed to like it though. He wanted to be a brave soldier and to become famous. Well, he certainly did both of those things."

In 1781, when he was 13 years old, a terrible thing happened. He was captured by the English army. "Bring that boy here!" the English commander said to his lieutenant. "I want to see if these upstart Americans teach their children any manners."

Grandpa George tried to sound English when he told the children what the officer said. This made Billy and Mary giggle even though they knew this was an exciting part of the story. He sounded so funny.

Andrew was brought from his cell and pushed roughly into the room. He frowned hard at the lieutenant. "All right, boy, what's your name?" the commander asked.

"My name is Andrew Jackson." Andrew stood up tall and straight and looked right at the English officer.

"Prisoner Jackson," the commander said, "you will call me sir."

Andrew said nothing. He just tried to frown a little harder and stand a little taller.

"You will learn your place, Prisoner Jackson," the commander went on. "My boots need polishing. Shine them."

"I will not!" Andrew almost shouted.

"What did you say?" The commander jumped to his feet.

"I said I won't shine your English boots," Andrew answered.

The English officer drew his sword. "I am going to punish you for that."

Andrew stood firm. He didn't even flinch. He just raised his hand as the officer swung his blade. The English commander hit Andrew with the flat of his sword. Even so, it cut deeply into his left hand and his left cheek. Andrew was taken back to his cell. He hadn't polished the commander's boots, but his refusal had cost him blood. He carried those scars with him the rest of his life. In most pictures of President Jackson, he has his head turned so that only the right side of his face is showing. He disliked the scar on his face and tried to hide it as often as possible. He never forgave the English for those scars. It was many years before he was able to get back at the English for that attack.

Several years after the American Revolution, the United States entered another war with England. By this time, Andrew Jackson was a general. In 1815, he was sent to the town of New Orleans in Louisiana. The English were going to try to capture the city. It was Jackson's job to keep them from doing it.

The two armies met in January. There were almost twice as many English soldiers as American ones. What was worse was that the English soldiers were well trained. Although the Americans were just volunteers, General Jackson wasn't too worried.

"I trust my boys," he said. "Those English have no real courage. They'll turn tail and run at the first shot we fire."

Jackson had his men pile bales of cotton to crouch behind. The cotton protected them from enemy bullets. The American soldiers were also able to surprise the English.

The plan worked. The English didn't turn around at the first shot, but neither did they stay and fight for long. General Andrew Jackson was called the Hero of New Orleans. The victory was all the sweeter for Jackson because he had finally been able to repay the English for his scars. It was because he was a brave hero that he was elected president.

"Was that the kind of story you wanted?" Grandpa asked.

"That was just right. Thank you," Billy replied.

Mary added, "Yes, thank you, Grandpa."

Their mother had been listening to Grandpa's story, too. She was inside the house in the living room. She could hear Grandpa through the open window. "Now, it's way past your bedtime, dears."

"Okay. We're coming," said Billy and Mary together. Bedtime was okay with them. It was late and they were both tired. They charged upstairs in nearly military fashion. Just before Billy fell asleep, he saw two fireflies. "I could have won the game," he said. "That would have been six." He wasn't awake long enough to be sad about it. 🌿

Billy Anderson's Think Box

❏ Why was such a young boy allowed to join the army?

❏ Later, what jobs did Andrew Jackson have?

❏ How did he get the reputation of being brave?

○ In what ways can you be brave while you are still a child? What are some of the things you would like to do when you are older?

○ By asking God to help us, can we learn to forgive others?

Thomas Jefferson

Declarer of Independence

"I don't want to fight a war," Mary complained.

"We have to," her brother, Billy, insisted.

Mary wasn't convinced. "Why do we have to?"

"Don't you know anything? That's the only way we'll be free," he answered. "Every country has had to fight for its independence. That's what the United States had to do."

"We did not," Mary said. "All we had to do was write the Declaration of Independence. We just told people we were free, and that made us free. Why don't we just write a declaration? Then we wouldn't have to fight a war."

Billy laughed. "Don't be silly. The United States wasn't free until we fought a war. The war was the important part. Anyway, the war is the fun part."

"Well, it's not the fun part for me," Mary said. "I'm not going to fight a war unless I find out I have to."

"All right," Billy answered, "let's go ask someone. You'll see. To be independent like America, we'll have to fight for it."

The two children looked for someone who could answer their questions. They found Grandpa George sitting on the porch with a newspaper and a cup of coffee.

Billy ran up to him so he could ask his question first. "Don't you always have to fight to be free?"

"I never had to," his grandfather answered, a little startled.

"That's not what I mean," Billy said.

"What do you mean, then?" Grandpa George peered over his paper.

"Mary and I are going to start a new country," Billy explained. "I think we have to fight a war. America wasn't a country until we fought a war, was it?"

"Well, sort of," Grandpa replied.

"But I don't want to fight a war," said Mary. "I thought the United States was a country as soon as they wrote the Declaration of Independence. Isn't that what July Fourth is all about? That's what Mom said."

"That's true, too," their grandfather said slowly.

"They can't both be right," complained Billy. "When were we really a new country?"

"Maybe I'd better tell you the story," said Grandpa. "It's two stories really. After that, you'll be able to decide how to start your own country."

The two children sat in front of Grandpa's chair to listen to his story which was really two stories.

The hero of the first part of our story is Thomas Jefferson. However, the story starts long before his part in it.

The United States started as a group of colonies from England. Even though the people who lived in America had left England, they still thought of themselves as English. Their children and their grandchildren felt the same way. America was just another place where Englishmen lived. The people still living in England also thought of the Americans as fellow citizens of England. Many of the laws in America were made in England.

You know that eventually the United States separated from England. Billy is right that a war had something to do with that. The war was called the American Revolution. However, right up to the time that the war started there were many people in America who didn't want independence from England. They may not have liked all of the laws made in England, but they still felt that the king of England was their king.

The real trouble started in 1760. That was when George III became king of England.

"That's your name, Grandpa," Mary said. "Were you named after the king of England?"

"I don't think so," her grandfather answered. "My father's name was George, and I was named after him. And before you ask, I don't think he was named after the king of England either. There are many people named George whose names have nothing to do with any kings."

When George III became king, England was fighting a war against France. War is expensive. Soldiers have to be paid. They need food, clothing, guns, and other things. England didn't have enough money to pay for the war. It was decided that the people living in America should help. England would get them to do this by charging new taxes on things like paper, tea, and glass. Every time someone in America would buy something that was taxed, they'd have to pay a little bit extra. The extra money would be sent to the English government so that it could pay for the war with France.

Taxes aren't always a bad thing. Today, most Americans pay taxes. Our government uses our tax money for many useful things. Some money is spent to make our roads safe, and some is spent to provide us with public libraries. There are many other ways our taxes are spent. The difference between our taxes and the ones made by England in those days is that we get to decide on the taxes we want. We elect people to Congress, and they make these decisions for us. However, it wasn't that way in King George's time. The colonists in America were taxed without a chance to decide whether they wanted to be taxed. That system was called "taxation without representation," and many people thought it was unfair.

The colonists protested the taxes. Some people, like Samuel Adams, decided the only answer was for America to be free from England. Other colonists only wanted the same rights as Englishmen who lived in

England. They wanted a voice in government and a chance to decide for themselves.

A meeting was held in the fall of 1774. It was called the First Continental Congress. The people who attended the meeting demanded to be given the same rights as other Englishmen. They were ignored.

The protests made King George angry. After all, he was the king. He didn't think people should argue with what he decided. He sent soldiers to America to make them pay the taxes. That made the Americans angrier. More and more of them decided they wanted to be independent.

In May of 1775, another meeting was held. This one was called, of course, the Second Continental Congress. Many of the greatest men in America went to this meeting. They hoped King George would change his mind and start treating them like other Englishmen. That was not the way things worked out. Just before the meeting started, a war between England and America began. English and American soldiers were shooting each other. The men at the Second Continental Congress realized that the king was not going to change his mind. Finally, they all understood that they would have to be free from England.

Five men were chosen for a very important job from all the people who attended the Second Continental Congress. Three of those men are still famous. They were Benjamin Franklin, John Adams, who became our second president, and Thomas Jefferson, who was our third president. Their job was to write a declaration of independence. The declaration explained why America should no longer be controlled by England. It showed why the English colonies in America wanted to become a free country called the United States.

The four other men chose Thomas Jefferson to write the declaration. Even though he was only thirty-two, he was already well known as a good writer. Jefferson thought that John Adams should write it. Adams was older than Thomas Jefferson and more experienced. Adams refused, saying, "I am suspected of being friendly to England. That makes me unpopular among the people of this fine country. And, anyway, you write ten times better than I can."

Jefferson agreed to write the declaration. He did a good job. I'm sure you've heard some of the words he wrote: "We hold these truths to be self-evident, that all men are created equal, that they are endowed by their Creator with certain unalienable Rights, that among these are Life, Liberty, and the pursuit of Happiness."

On July 4, 1776, the Second Continental Congress voted unanimously to approve Jefferson's declaration. As far as they were concerned, they were then free from England. Riders were hired to travel all over the colonies to read the Declaration. Everywhere people heard it, they celebrated. They were free! They were part of a brand new country.

"So, America did become a country without having a war," Mary said smugly.

"Sort of," said Grandpa George.

"But you just said they were free as soon as they wrote the Declaration of Independence," Mary said.

"They thought they were free," Grandpa said, "but England didn't think so. It's one thing to call yourself free; it's another thing to prove it."

"They proved it with a war, didn't they?" asked Billy.

"In part," said their grandfather. "That's the next part of our story. I'll tell that to you after lunch, okay?"

"You promise?" asked Mary.

"I promise." 🌿

Mary Anderson's Think Box

❑ Why was King George angry?

❑ Is it important for people to pay taxes? Do you and your parents pay taxes?

❑ Read two things Jesus said about paying taxes: Matthew 17:24–27 and 22:15–22. What was his advice to us concerning taxes?

❑ Why was the Declaration of Independence important? Did Thomas Jefferson do a good job in writing it? Was he an old man when he wrote it?

❑ What does it mean to have "a voice" in government?

○ It is best to try to solve problems in a peaceful way. In what ways can you help solve problems in your family?

James Madison
Father of the Constitution

"**B**ut you promised," Billy complained.

"I know," said Grandpa George.

"You said you would tell us the rest of the story about how we became the United States," Billy reminded him.

"I'm still going to tell you the story," his grandfather replied. "This doesn't mean that I'm not going to tell you the story. I simply forgot about your trip to the dentist this afternoon."

"But we need to know now," said Mary. "We were going to start our country today. We can't do that until we hear the end of your story."

"Your mother won't want to cancel your dental appointments just so I can finish this story," Grandpa said. "I could come with you, though. I could tell you the story in the car on the way to the dentist. How would that be?"

The children agreed that if they couldn't avoid seeing the dentist, hearing Grandpa's story in the car was the next best thing.

"Do you remember what I told you this morning?" Grandpa asked when everyone was settled in the car.

"Maybe you had better start with that part just to make sure," Billy said.

At first, the people living in America didn't want to be free. They were Englishmen. The king of England was their king. The laws of England were their laws. Then when England started treating them unfairly, they protested the new laws and new taxes. That made King George III angry. He sent soldiers to America to make people pay the taxes. The Americans saw that England was never going to treat them fairly. If they wanted a fair government, they would have to make it themselves. They decided to be a new, free country so they could make their own laws.

The king of England saw what was happening. He didn't want America to be free. He liked owning America. There were many valuable things in America that he could use as long as he still controlled it. He could also make a lot of money as long as all the Americans paid him taxes. He decided to fight to keep them from being free. Not long after the war started, Thomas Jefferson wrote the Declaration of Independence.

From that time on, the Americans thought of themselves as free. They were then the United States. They were a brand new country. However, England didn't think of them that way yet. America would have to prove that it was its own country. Most people thought winning the war against England would be proof enough. As hard as it was to win, though, they would have to do more than that to be a real country.

The American Revolution started in 1775 when British soldiers attacked American minutemen at Lexington and Concord. The British had gone to these towns for two reasons. One was to capture Sam Adams and John Hancock. The other was to destroy a collection of guns and ammunition the Americans had been saving in case war started. Minutemen were America's only soldiers. It didn't have a trained army. The minutemen were private citizens: farmers and shopkeepers. They brought their own guns to the battlefield wherever soldiers were needed. They were called minutemen because whenever the call for troops went out, they were there in a minute.

The first shot fired by American minutemen at Lexington was called "the shot heard around the world." It wasn't really that loud. It was named that because it was so important. That was the first step America took in its fight to be free.

The American Revolution lasted a long time. It didn't end until 1781. That was six years later. The English had no idea that it would last that long. It shouldn't have, and America shouldn't have won. England was a very strong country. Its army was large and well-trained. America didn't even have an army when the war started. England had a large navy that was feared by the whole world. America didn't have a navy at all. It had only merchant ships for trading with other countries. What America had was people with a fierce determination to be free. America won the war because its people believed in liberty. Many brave men and women fought for that belief.

Many people in America had thought that winning the war would be enough. "Once we win the war," they said, "we will be a free country. Nobody will be able to say that we aren't the United States of America." They were wrong. It was true that England didn't control America anymore. However, few people had stopped to ask who was going to rule America once the British were gone. What kind of country would it be? What kind of government would it have?

America first tried to answer these questions in 1781. The answer was a plan called the Articles of Confederation. Meetings were held for four years before all the states agreed to the Articles. However, the Articles of Confederation were not the right answer to America's questions. The plan didn't work because no one was really in control. It may sound strange, but the problem was too much freedom.

Everyone wanted to be free. Each state even wanted to be its own country. You can imagine how confusing that was. There was a country of Virginia and a country of New York and so on.

"Was our state its own country?" Mary asked.

"No," answered Grandpa, "our state wasn't even a state yet."

Each state had its own money and its own laws. If you were from New Jersey, you couldn't buy anything in Connecticut because they wouldn't take foreign money.

That system couldn't last. America had been strong enough to beat England only because all of the states worked together. Each state was not strong enough or rich enough to be a country by itself. They needed a new plan. They needed a new answer to what kind of government would make us a strong country that would last.

In 1786, a message went out to all of the states. The next year there would be another meeting. This meeting was called to fix the Articles of Confederation. In May of 1787, the delegates began to arrive in Philadelphia. Only Rhode Island didn't send delegates. They were still determined to be their own country.

George Washington was elected to preside over the meeting. He was a great war hero. He had led America to victory over the English.

It didn't take long for everyone at the meeting to figure out they could not fix the Articles of Confederation. The Articles were too bad. "We should have formed a government when we wrote the Declaration of Independence," some people said. "All the states wanted to work together then. We wouldn't have all these separate countries if we had agreed to stay together at that time."

The delegates had to come up with a whole new idea. This is where James Madison came in. He is the hero of the second part of this story. You can think of it this way. Thomas Jefferson started the United States of America. He explained why we should be free. From the time that the Declaration of Independence was written, we thought of ourselves as a free country. We could make our own decisions about how we would be governed. James Madison completed the United States. We still use the decisions he made. The government of our country is the way it is because of him.

James Madison wrote a great document. It is called the Constitution. It describes how our government works. Madison is known as the "Father of the Constitution." The Constitution says that we should have a Congress with two parts, the Senate and the House of Representatives. It says that we should have one President to govern all of the states. It also says that we should have a Supreme Court to judge whether our laws are fair. More than two hundred years later, we are still using Madison's ideas.

However, Madison's ideas weren't enough. People wanted certain laws put into the Constitution as well. They still remembered the way their rights had been taken away by England. They thought that if those rights were put into the Constitution then they would be permanent.

Part of the Constitution described the way to add laws. These laws are called amendments. James Madison wrote the first ten amendments to the Constitution. These ten laws are called the Bill of Rights. The First Amendment says Americans are free to believe or say anything they want. The Second Amendment states that the people have the right to defend themselves. Other amendments promise the right to privacy and make sure that the courts of law act fairly.

Just then Mom pulled the car into the parking lot at the dentist's office.

"Is there a law in the Constitution about going to the dentist?" Billy asked.

"No, there isn't," Mother spoke up. "Freedom from dental visits is not one of our sacred rights."

"Have my stories answered your questions, kids?" Grandpa asked.

"I guess," said Billy. "I'm still going to be in charge of fighting the war."

"But I don't have to fight," Mary said with a smile. "I'm going to write our Declaration of Independence and our Constitution." 🌾

❏ Who were the minutemen? How did they get that name?

❏ Why do you think the Revolutionary War lasted so long?

❏ Did the people of America have problems when they were free? What happened?

❏ What is the name of the important document which James Madison wrote?

○ When people are "free," does it mean that they do not have laws? All countries need rules and laws. Parents have rules for their homes, too. What are some of the rules in your home? What are God's rules? Did God make rules to help us be happy?

George Washington

The Reluctant President

There was a knock on the door. Billy's mother, Susan Anderson, answered it. It was Billy's Uncle Bob.

"Where's Billy?" he asked. "It's almost time for me to take him to his soccer tryouts."

"I don't think he wants to go anymore," Billy's mother answered. "He's in his room now."

"Why doesn't he want to go?"

"I don't know. You'll have to ask him," Mrs. Anderson said.

Uncle Bob went to Billy's room and knocked on the door.

Billy called out, "Who is it?"

"It's me, Billy, Uncle Bob. May I come in and talk to you?"

"Sure. Come on in." Billy was on his bed reading a book. He put the book down as Bob came in and sat on the bed next to him.

"Do you still want to go to the soccer tryouts?" Uncle Bob asked.

"No, thank you," Billy answered. "I've decided not to try out."

"Why is that, William? Is something wrong?"

Billy liked it when Uncle Bob called him William. His mother only called him that when he had done something wrong. With his uncle it was different. When Uncle Bob called him William, it made him feel quite grown up. He decided he could talk to Uncle Bob about what was bothering him.

Billy frowned. "I don't know how well I can play. I don't know whether I'll make the team."

"That reminds me of a story about George Washington," Uncle Bob said.

"Is this the story about cutting down the cherry tree?" Billy liked all of Uncle Bob's stories, but he especially liked that one because it showed that even someone like George Washington got into trouble sometimes.

"No," said Uncle Bob, "that story is about telling the truth. You already know how to do that. This is the story about how George Washington wasn't sure he wanted to be the first president of the United States."

"Really? He didn't want to be president? But why?" Billy asked.

"Well, you listen to the story, and you'll find out."

Early in April of 1789, a messenger came from New York City to George Washington's farm at Mount Vernon, Virginia.

"Mr. Washington," he announced, "you have been chosen by the people of this country to be the first president of the United States. You are a hero, sir. You led them through the revolution, and they want you to continue to lead them."

"I told the people of this great nation that I didn't want another public office," Washington answered a little sadly. "All I wanted to do was to settle down and work on my farm. However, since the people have asked me to take this position, I will."

Washington wasn't happy about being chosen. He had been the general in charge of the American troops during the Revolution. It was partly because of him that the

United States was a free country. He knew that he could be a general, but he didn't know if he could be a president. He had never been a president before. In fact, no one had.

At that time, the federal government was in New York City. Washington, D. C., where the government is now, was not even built yet. There weren't any cars either. They hadn't been invented yet. So Washington had to go all the way from Virginia to New York in a coach drawn by horses.

All along the road, at every town or village, the people turned out to cheer for their new president. Washington was traveling with his old friend, Colonel David Humphreys. The president told his friend, "David, all this cheering doesn't make me happy. I am afraid that I am going to let these people down. I am afraid that I will not be a good president." No matter what Colonel Humphreys said, he couldn't make George Washington feel any better.

Eight days after leaving Virginia, they arrived in New York City. When George Washington reached the capital, the mayor of New York City and the governor of New York State gave him a party. At last, it was almost time for the president to go to work. First, he had to take the oath of office. The oath is a promise a president makes to do the best he can. Finally, it was time to find out how good his best was.

As you probably already know, George Washington's best was very good, indeed. He had to make hundreds of decisions about how our government would work. He had to decide everything from how many advisors the president should have to how many times he could visit the Congress. Our first president even decided to be president only twice. Almost every president since then has made the same decision. George Washington did so well that many of the decisions he made have become permanent parts of our government.

"George Washington was one of our greatest presidents even though he didn't think he would be. How well he did is not the most important part of this story. Do you know what is important about this story, William?"

Billy knew that his uncle's stories were different from the ones Grandpa George told him. Both of them told interesting stories, but Uncle Bob's stories were also meant to teach a lesson. Billy was ready for his uncle's question.

"The important thing is that George Washington tried to be a good president even though he didn't know if he could," Billy said. Uncle Bob smiled. Billy was happy that he had figured out the lesson Uncle Bob was trying to teach him.

"That's right, Billy. Very good. Now do you want to follow his lead and give soccer a try?" Bob asked.

"Yes. I'm ready to go now. I guess it will be okay even if I don't make the team," Billy said.

"Of course it will be, because you'll have tried. Hurry up and get ready to go, or we'll be late." Uncle Bob got up and clapped his hands.

They were soon rushing out of the house and into Uncle Bob's car. They reached the tryouts just in time. And Billy did make the team! ✺

Uncle Bob Anderson's Think Box

❑ What did George Washington want to do instead of being president?

❑ Was George Washington a good president? Why?

○ Was George Washington afraid of doing hard things he had never done before? Did he do his best or did he refuse to try? What do you think you should do when you are asked to try to do something hard or new? Will you feel happy when you have done your very best?

John Adams

Treasure Hunter

Mary was the first to finish her dinner. She had a special project she wanted to work on. Her parents excused her from the table, and she went into the living room to wait for her brother, Billy, to finish eating.

It seemed to Mary that it took Billy a long time to eat his dinner. She had a new puzzle that she wanted her brother to help her with. When he finally finished and was allowed to leave the table, Mary followed him to his room.

"Come help me with my puzzle, Billy," Mary said.

"No. I'm going to play ball with Tom," he answered.

"If you don't help me, I won't be able to do it," Mary complained.

"Then you just won't be able to do it." Billy left to find Tom.

Mary went to her room and started to cry. She wanted to put her puzzle together, but she was sure she needed help. Aunt Anne heard her crying and called to her to come downstairs.

Mary took her puzzle with her to the living room. Maybe someone down there could help her. "Now, tell us what's the matter," said Aunt Anne as she helped Mary onto her lap.

"Yes," said Uncle Bob, leaning over and patting her head. "What's so bad that your pretty face is all wet with tears?"

"It's Billy. He won't help me put my new puzzle together."

"Can't you put it together by yourself?" asked Aunt Anne.

"No. It's new. I've never done it before. I don't know how," Mary almost started to cry again. It didn't seem that anyone wanted to help her.

"You've done other puzzles, haven't you?" Aunt Anne asked.

"Sure. I love to do puzzles, but no one will help me with this one." She started to frown again.

"You know, Mary," Uncle Bob said, "you sound a bit like the second president of the United States, John Adams."

"How do you know what he sounded like? He lived a long time ago, didn't he?" Mary asked. She'd almost forgotten her puzzle.

"Yes, Bob, how do you know what he sounded like?" Aunt Anne asked.

"Well, I never heard him in person, of course, Mary," Uncle Bob said, ignoring Aunt Anne. "However, your great-great-grandfather was a friend of many of our founding fathers. Or maybe it was your great-great-great-grandfather. John Adams told him this story himself, and it has been passed down through our family ever since.

When Adams was still a young man in school, he felt the same way you do now. He once wrote, "It is my destiny to dig treasures with my own fingers. Nobody will lend me or sell me a pick axe."

"Do you know what he meant by that?"

Mary said, "It sounds like he wanted to dig holes and no one would help him."

"That's not quite what he meant." Bob explained, "The treasures that he was talking about are the good things that he wanted to do. We all have those kinds of treasures. Your treasures are the beautiful pictures you've made for us or the books you've read."

"Or putting my new puzzle together," Mary said.

"That's right. All the good things that you can do or the nice things you do for other people," Aunt Anne said.

"What John Adams meant," Uncle Bob went on, "was that he thought he would have to do all his good things without help. The kind of help he wanted, when he wrote that, was to have friends who could give him a job as a lawyer. However, he didn't know anybody like that. So what do you think he did?"

Mary shrugged. "I don't know."

"From what he said you can tell that he didn't give up."

He knew it was going to be hard. It was going to be just as hard as digging holes without a pick axe or a shovel. However, he did it anyway. One of the things he did was to train himself to be the best lawyer he could be. Since no one was giving him a job, he decided to be such a good lawyer that someone would have to hire him. To do this, he studied ancient law a certain amount of time every day. He did the same with modern law. He also studied foreign languages at certain times of every day. In the end, he became a good lawyer. He did it by working hard and not worrying about help.

By working hard, John Adams became a leader of the United States even before we were a country. He fought and argued for the rights of the people of this country. That's how he became our first vice president and then our second president. That was after George Washington, of course.

"Now, what is the most important part of the John Adams' story?" Uncle Bob usually asked that question after he told a story.

Mary knew the answer. "Not to give up when we don't have help. We can all dig our treasures."

"And what does that mean?" Bob asked.

"It means we can all do good things if we try," Mary said, smiling.

"Very good. And now what are you going to do?" asked Aunt Anne.

"I'm going to work on my puzzle by myself!"

"That's a good idea," Anne said, "but don't be afraid to ask for help if you need it. It's not bad to need some help sometimes. We just shouldn't give up if we don't get any."

Mary climbed down from Aunt Anne's lap and went right to work on the puzzle. She only needed help with a couple of pieces. When it was finished, she had a picture of a treasure chest full of pretty things. ❧

Aunt Anne Anderson's Think Box

❑ What did John Adams do when he found things were hard and he did not have a job?

❑ What job did he get after he became good lawyer?

○ Do you have something you would like to do but find hard? Think about how you can work hard without giving up even when you feel like quitting.

Eli Whitney

Mr. Fix-It

Mary woke up curious. Sometimes she did that. She would just wake up and everything she saw would put questions into her head.

That's how it was this morning. Everything she saw or touched or smelled was like a question waiting to be asked. Everything was a puzzle waiting to be solved. Well, almost everything. Whenever it happened, Mary would go to her mother to get the answers. One day, her mother finally told her that she had too many questions for one person to answer. She said that Mary had to pick one question to ask at a time. So this morning as she got up, she listed the questions. She wanted to pick the very best one.

The first thing she saw was the sun coming in through the window, but that was no good. Mary thought the sun was very good, really. However, it wouldn't work as her question for this morning. She had already asked her mother about the sun. She had even asked about windows already.

When she pushed the sheet and covers back and climbed out of bed, she noticed her bed. Then she looked at her dresser where she kept her clothes neatly folded. Those things were no good for questions either. She had already heard how furniture is made. She even knew about forests and lumber and the wood that is used to make furniture.

She dressed in her favorite red pants and green shirt. She liked this outfit even though her mother said they didn't go together.

She started to go downstairs feeling very proud of herself. She knew quite a lot, maybe everything. She had not seen anything yet that she had to ask her mother about.

Then, suddenly, she stopped. She hadn't thought about seeing her curtains. She hadn't thought about seeing her sheets and blankets. She hadn't thought about seeing her clothes as she put them on. She didn't know about any of these things.

She rushed to find her mother and ask her about these things. Mary found her in the dining room. Her mother was drinking coffee and reading the newspaper. "Good morning, Mommy. I have a question for you," Mary said. She sat down at her place at the table.

Her mother leaned across and kissed her. "Good morning, my precious. And what is puzzling you today?"

"Where do curtains and sheets and blankets and clothes come from?" Mary asked her question very quickly. She knew she could only ask one question, but she was curious about everything she had seen.

"Well," answered her mother, "that's a long question. However, I think I can answer the whole thing with just one story.

"I'm going to tell you the story of cotton and how we came to use so much of it," Mary's mother began. "There is cotton in everything you asked about. It is partly because of an invention by a man named Eli Whitney that we make so many things out of cotton."

Eli Whitney was born on a farm in Massachusetts in 1765. When he was born,

America wasn't even a country yet. The states were still colonies of England.

Eli wasn't interested in farming. He avoided doing his chores whenever he could. His father would often find him building something in the workshop. "Tinkering around again, Eli?" his father would ask.

"Yes, sir," Eli would answer, a little embarrassed.

"You know, it's not fair to your brothers and sisters that they should have to do your share of the chores as well as their own," Eli's father would point out to him.

"I know, Pa, but I almost have this fixed," Eli would sometimes say. Other times he would answer, "I really think I've got a good idea. This will make all of our work easier."

"What would make our work easier," his father would complain, "is your doing your own share of the farming. Now get out to the fields."

Eli Whitney would go back to farming for a little while. It wouldn't be long, though, before he would be back in the workshop. Some people are just born to do certain things. Eli was born to build and fix things.

"You, my little precious, were born to ask questions." Mary's mother smiled at her, and Mary grinned back.

After he finished college, Eli got a teaching job in Georgia. On the train traveling to it, he met Mrs. Greene, who owned a plantation in Georgia. A plantation is a very large farm. She invited Eli to stay with her for a short while on her farm. This was a good thing for Eli because before he could get to his new teaching job, it was given to someone else.

Just as he had done on his family's farm in Massachusetts, Eli fixed and made things on Mrs. Greene's plantation. Mrs. Greene was impressed. It seemed that anything Eli could imagine, he could build.

One day some other farmers were at Mrs. Greene's place. They complained about how expensive it was to grow cotton. "It takes one of my slaves ten hours to prepare just one pound of cotton," one of the farmers said.

"What do you have to do to prepare the cotton?" Mrs. Greene asked.

"The fluffy cotton fibers have to be pulled away from the little hard seeds," the farmer explained. "If we only had a machine that could do it faster, I'm sure we could make a lot of money."

"Tell young Eli Whitney your problems," Mrs. Greene said. "He can make anything mechanical. I'm sure he can help you."

The farmers did just that. Not long after they had told him about their problems, they came back to see how things were going. "Eli, can we come in and see what you're doing?" asked the farmers, knocking on the workroom door.

"Sure, come on in. I have something to show you." Eli showed them a small version of his invention.

The farmers were amazed. He had solved their problem. "It's only been two weeks, Eli," they said, "and you already have a model of your new machine! What is it called?"

"It's a cotton gin. It pulls the cotton through a piece of screen wire. The seeds are left on one side and the fluffy cotton fiber comes out the other side."

"You're a genius," one farmer exclaimed. The others agreed with him.

Soon Eli Whitney had built a large version of his cotton gin. It could prepare between three hundred and one thousand pounds of cotton fiber in a single day. That was much faster than doing it by hand.

Eli's machine meant that southern farmers could grow much more cotton. They didn't have to worry any more about preparing it. That part was easy. Soon everybody wanted to use cotton. They made all sorts of things from it.

"Like curtains and sheets and clothes," said Mary.

"That's right," her mother nodded. "They even make red pants and green shirts that don't go together."

Mary laughed. She jumped down from her chair and ran off. She wanted to find everything in the house that was made of cotton.

Katherine Anderson's Think Box

❏ Where did Eli prefer to spend his time?

❏ Why was cotton so important in those days? Why is it important now?

❏ What did Eli Whitney invent that helped the farmers? How did it work?

O What would you like to invent?

Lewis & Clark
Journals for Jefferson

❝I discovered all sorts of things," Mary said excitedly.

"Then you had a good time at Grandma and Grandpa Anderson's?" her mother asked.

"I had the best time!" Mary and her brother, Billy, had spent the weekend at their grandparents' farm not too far outside the city where they lived. There was a large forest behind the farmhouse. The children often explored in the woods. Exploring was one of the best parts about visiting the farm.

Now they were driving home, and Mary had so much to tell her parents while Billy was asleep in the seat next to her. She wanted to tell her parents about their weekend now, because if Billy was awake he might take credit for some of the things they had found.

"What did you discover?" Mary's father asked.

"I saw a beautiful bird. I've never seen one like it before," she answered.

"What did it look like?"

Mary described the bird. "Well, it was blue on top and gray underneath. And it had black and white bits on its wings."

"New discoveries are often named for the person who finds them. Maybe we should name this bird after you," Dad suggested.

"You should paint a picture of the Mary Bird for me when we get home." Mother said. "Then, I'll know just how it looks."

"Okay, Mom, I can do that." Mary was very happy about having a bird named for her.

"Did you find anything else?" her father asked.

"I also found a little bush. It had hard leaves that were dark green on top, but almost white underneath. It also had little red berries."

"That must be a Mary Berry Bush." Mary and her father both laughed at her mother's suggestion.

"If you're going to keep finding so many things, you'll need a journal," her father said.

"What's a journal?" Mary wanted to know.

Mary's mother explained. "It's like a notebook. You can write down everything interesting that you find or that happens to you. You can even draw pictures of the things you see so that you won't forget what they look like. Many famous explorers have written journals about their trips and their discoveries."

"Shall I tell you the story of the famous explorers Lewis and Clark?" Father asked. "They knew how important a set of journals could be."

"Yes, please." Mary settled back in the car seat.

In 1801, when Thomas Jefferson became our third president, the western part of the United States had hardly been explored. Few Americans had been west of the Mississippi River. This was because the land didn't belong to the United States. Much of it belonged to France. England and Spain also owned parts of it. But Jefferson was very interested in the West.

Two years later, in 1803, Jefferson got his chance to find out what lay west of the Mississippi River. In that year, he bought the land between the Mississippi and the Rocky Mountains from France. It was called the Louisiana Territory, although it was much larger than the modern state of Louisiana.

The first thing to do was to explore this new land. Jefferson wanted to know all about the territory he had just purchased. He called on a young army officer named Meriwether Lewis. The Jeffersons and the Lewises had lived near each other in Virginia, and Thomas Jefferson already knew young Captain Lewis.

"I have a important mission for you," President Jefferson said.

"I will do anything my president and my country ask of me," answered Meriwether Lewis.

"I want you to explore the Louisiana Territory. Find out if there is a river that flows from the Mississippi River to the Pacific Ocean. Also, find out about the animals, plants, and people which live in this new land. I want a full report of everything you find."

"I will do my best, sir. I think it would be a good idea to take along another leader, as well. That way, if something happens to one of us, the report you want can still be made by the other," Lewis suggested.

"Do you have any ideas as to who you would want to take with you?" Thomas Jefferson asked.

"I would like to take William Clark. He is a friend of mine from the army. He is very capable and would serve you well."

"Very well," the president said, "take this Clark with you as well as whatever men and supplies you will need."

"Thank you, sir," Meriwether Lewis said.

Jefferson smiled. "It is I who should thank you for what you are going to do. The whole country will thank you if you are successful and if you bring back the reports I have asked you to make."

By May of 1804, Lewis and Clark were ready to set out on their trip. They had gathered a party of about forty men. Some of these men were soldiers, and some were scouts who were familiar with the land through which they would be traveling. The group was called the Corps of Discovery.

They spent all of that summer and part of the fall traveling up the Missouri River. This part of the trip wasn't easy for them because the river was flowing against them. They saw many plants and animals which were unfamiliar to them. They saw huge herds of buffalo and antelope. They saw a strange animal that lived in holes in the ground. Lewis called these animals "barking squirrels." We now call them prairie dogs.

The Corps of Discovery also met many Indian tribes that they hadn't known about. Most of these tribes were friendly. They offered Lewis and Clark food and places to stay.

When winter came, the river became too icy to travel. Lewis and Clark built a fort near one of the friendly Indian tribes named the Mandan Indians. They sent some men from the Corps of Discovery back down the river. These men were to deliver the first volumes of the journals of Lewis and Clark to the president. These men were replaced by scouts who were also visiting the Mandans. One of the new scouts had an Indian wife named Sacagawea. She was not a Mandan. Her tribe lived in the Rocky Mountains. Lewis and Clark thought she would be helpful when they had to cross those mountains so they let her join the Corps of Discovery.

When spring came, Lewis and Clark continued their journey. They hoped to get all the way to the Pacific Ocean and back to their camp with the Mandans before the next winter. They weren't able to do it. It was much harder to get through the Rocky Mountains than they had thought it would be. Even with Sacagawea's help, it took a long time. They just made it to the Pacific Ocean when winter set in again. They stayed on the coast in another fort that they built.

Their journals were always the most important thing to them. They wanted everyone to know what they had found. They knew that ships from England and the United

States had been to the part of the coast where they were staying. They planned to send some more of their journals back to President Jefferson in one of these ships. But no boats landed there that winter.

Finally, when spring came again they turned around and headed home. Going back East was much easier than it had been to get to the Pacific Ocean. Now, the Corps of Discovery had many Indian friends to help them. Also, the Missouri River flowed in the direction they were headed.

Lewis and Clark got back to St. Louis in September of 1806. They had been gone almost two and a half years. Some people had thought they wouldn't make it. Others thought that something had happened to them on their trip. Everyone was happy when they returned.

"Do you know the most important thing that Lewis and Clark brought back?" Mary's father asked.

"Their notebooks," said Mary.

Father smiled and nodded. "That's right. Those journals contained information about plants, animals, and people that most people living in the United States had never seen. Their notebooks made it much easier for all the people who traveled to the West after they did. So what do you think? Should we get you a notebook that you can use as a journal when you visit your grandparents' house?"

"Oh, yes, please!" Mary bounced on the car seat. "I'm sure there are lots of discoveries I could make."

"Now if you could only be a little more like Meriwether Lewis, " Mother said. "If only you would be happy to do anything your parents or your country asked of you, like clean your room."

"Oh, Mom," Mary giggled, "why would the country ask me to clean my room?" 🌿

Richard Anderson's Think Box

❑ President Jefferson wanted someone to explore the western part of the United States. Whom did he choose?

❑ Lewis and Clark wrote and drew illustrations in their journals. What were some of the things they wrote about?

○ What if Lewis or Clark had said, "I don't like to write in journals?" Do you think they could have remembered everything they did and saw? Writing is sometimes hard work but it is important work. Writing made a permanent record of things that Lewis and Clark did and saw.

Sacagawea

The Indian Guide

"That's right, little grasshopper. You just sit there. I'm not going to hurt you." Mary spoke quietly to the tiny bug she had found. She was lying on her stomach in her back yard. She was carefully drawing a picture of the grasshopper in her new journal.

Mary had just finished drawing the big jumping legs of the grasshopper when Billy came running up. "What are you doing, Mary?"

The noise frightened the grasshopper and it jumped away. "Now you've ruined it!" Mary complained. "I was trying to draw that grasshopper in my journal."

"Why were you doing that?"

"I'm practicing being an explorer," Mary explained. "The first thing I was going to do was to draw every kind of bug we have in our yard."

"That's silly," Billy laughed. "Girls aren't explorers."

Mary tossed her head. "Sure, they are. I'm going to be one."

"That doesn't count. You're not one yet," Billy grinned. "Tell me about a girl that has been an explorer. I'll bet you can't!"

Mary couldn't remember any, but she wasn't going to let Billy win this argument. "I think Mom can tell us the story of a girl explorer."

"And I think she can't, because they're aren't any," Billy said.

"Come on. Let's ask her." Mary picked up her journal as they hurried to the house.

They found their mother in the living room. "There aren't any girl explorers, are there?" Billy asked. "Mary wants to be one, but I told her there's no such thing."

"I'm afraid you're wrong, Billy," Mom replied. "Would you like to hear the story of a famous woman who was also an important explorer?"

"Yes, please!" Mary made a face at Billy who sat down with a frown to hear the story.

"Do you remember Daddy's story about Lewis and Clark?" Mom asked.

"Yes. I remember," said Mary.

Billy looked confused. "I don't remember that story. When did Daddy tell it?"

"He told it on the way back from Grandma and Grandpa Anderson's house," Mary told him. "You were asleep because all of our exploring wore you out. I didn't need to sleep. I guess that shows that girls are better explorers."

"It does not," Billy argued.

"Yes, it does."

"All right, you two. This isn't a time to argue. This is a time to listen to a story," their mother said.

"When Daddy told that story," she went on, "he mentioned a young Indian woman named Sacagawea. She was an important part of the journey of Lewis and Clark. But she had led a busy life even before she met Lewis and Clark and their Corps of Discovery."

Sacagawea was born a Shoshone Indian. The Shoshones lived in the Rocky Mountains. A few years before Lewis and Clark traveled from the Mississippi River to the Pacific

Ocean, Sacagawea was kidnapped from her home. She and other members of her tribe were taken by a group of Hidatsa Indians. The Hidatsa tribe lived in what is now called North Dakota.

While Sacagawea was living with the Hidatsas, she met and became the wife of a French Canadian named Toussaint Charbonneau.

Billy made a face. He didn't like mushy stuff in his stories. His mother poked him gently in the stomach, tickling him. He giggled and then settled down to hear the rest of the story. Mommy continued.

Charbonneau was a trader. He gave the Indians cloth, beads, and tools in return for furs. He knew much about the land between the Hidatsa villages and the Rocky Mountains. He also knew many of the Indian tribes in that area and their languages.

In the fall of 1804, Lewis and Clark and their Corps of Discovery arrived in the area. They stayed with the Mandan Indians who were neighbors of the Hidatsas. Some of the men of the Corps of Discovery were sent back down the Missouri River, the way they had just come. Lewis and Clark sent some of their journals with these men. The explorers didn't know what would happen to them and they wanted President Jefferson to have all the information they had gathered.

Lewis and Clark needed to hire new scouts to take the place of the men they had sent home. A scout had to know the land through which the Corps of Discovery would be traveling and be able to communicate with the Indians. One of the men Lewis and Clark chose was Charbonneau. That winter, while the explorers were staying in their camp with the Mandan Indians, Sacagawea had a son. Charbonneau didn't want to leave his wife or his newborn son, Jean Baptiste. He went to see Lewis and Clark. "Sirs," Charbonneau said, "I would like to bring my wife and young son on our journey."

Meriwether Lewis was doubtful. "I don't know. A woman, especially a woman with a child, is sure to slow us down."

"She can be a great help to you," insisted Charbonneau. "She is from the Shoshone people who live in the Rocky Mountains. They will help you a great deal if she is with us."

"I hope you are right," said William Clark. "Bring her along."

The next spring, the whole group left the Mandan camp and headed west. When they reached the Rocky Mountains, they found out that Charbonneau had been right. The chief of the Shoshone Indians was named Cameahwiat. He was Sacagawea's brother.

Cameahwait was happy to see his sister again after so many years. He had not known what had happened to her. He was also pleased with young Jean Baptiste. He gave the Corps of Discovery some horses and a guide to lead them safely on their way even though he didn't trust the explorers.

However, Sacagawea was not only important to Lewis and Clark because of whom she knew. She also proved herself to be brave and smart.

It was easier to travel on the rivers than to hike along the shore. Lewis and Clark traveled by canoe as often as possible. One day, a strong wind blew one of the canoes on its side. Charbonneau fell out of the canoe and so did many of their supplies. The canoe filled with water and almost sank before they reached the shore of the river. Sacagawea was the hero of the day. She stayed calm in the canoe. With little Jean Baptiste on one arm, she caught many of the items that had washed overboard and scooped them back into the canoe.

"We would have had a hard time getting all the way to the Pacific Ocean without your quick thinking," Lewis told her. "I'm glad that we brought you along." Both Sacagawea and Charbonneau smiled proudly at these words.

When Lewis and Clark finished their mission, Sacagawea did not return with them to the East to see President Jefferson. She and her family stayed in the Hidatsa village where she and Charbonneau had met. Lewis and Clark were sorry to have to part with this remarkable woman.

"So you see, women can make good explorers. They can be just as brave and smart as anyone," Mom finished.

"Thanks for the story, Mom. So Billy, I was right!" Mary said. "I'm going to go back and work on my journal."

"Can I help?" asked Billy.

Mary nodded. "Sure. We can find bugs together, if you don't step on them first!" 🌿

Mary Anderson's Think Box

❑ Why did Meriwether Lewis decide to take Sacagawea on their journey?

❑ What did she do that proved she was a good explorer?

❑ To be an explorer you should be brave. What are some of the other character traits that would be helpful?

◯ What kind of exploration can you do?

Robert Fulton

Steamboat Builder

"Hey! Stop splashing me!" Billy yelled.

"I'm not splashing you," Mary exclaimed.

"Dad! Make her stop splashing me. She's ruining my sailboat!"

Father came over to see what was going on.

Mary looked up at him. "I didn't do it on purpose. I was just kicking my feet."

"Well, Mary, please be more careful," Father said. "Even without Mary's help, you haven't been having much luck with your boat, Billy."

"Yeah, I know," Billy groaned as they all watched the boat tip over, fill with water, and sink. Billy fished his sailboat out of the water. He sat down at the edge of the pond and looked at his shoes.

That morning their father had shown Billy and Mary how to fold newspapers into the shape of sailboats. Billy was now trying to get one to float across the pond in the park. As his father had said, he wasn't having much luck. He had tried so often that he was nearly out of newspaper.

"Are you going to give up on your project?" Billy's father asked.

"I don't know. Maybe," Billy mumbled.

"Maybe you shouldn't quit just yet. There's still some more newspaper. While you're thinking about it, maybe you'd like to hear a story. I know one about another ship builder. His first tries sank, too." Billy's father smiled at him and ruffled his hair.

Billy brightened a little. "Okay," he said. "I'd like to hear that one."

This is the story of Robert Fulton. He was the first man to build a steamboat that worked well. A steamboat could go much faster than a sailboat, and it didn't matter if the wind was blowing. After Robert Fulton's invention, many people began to travel by steamboat. It was very popular.

One thing about Fulton's steamboat was that he didn't actually invent it. Other people had been trying to build a boat that would be powered by steam. Fulton took all these other attempts and combined them with ideas of his own. He didn't invent the steamboat; he just figured out how to make one that would work.

Robert Fulton was born in a small town called Little Britain, in Pennsylvania, in 1765. When he was still a boy, his father died and the family moved to Lancaster, Pennsylvania. Lancaster was a much more interesting place for young Robert. It was a larger city with many more things to explore. Best of all, there was a factory near his home. He watched weapons being made for the American troops fighting the Revolutionary War.

Robert had always been curious. He spent many afternoons standing by the factory doors watching the work being done. When the factory workers came close enough, he would ask them questions about their work. Robert was liked by all of the workers in the factory because he asked such good questions. It wasn't long before he was allowed to wander through the factory.

When he was not studying the machines at the weapons factory, Robert was painting. He would often walk a short way out of town to paint the landscape.

As Robert grew older, he realized how poor his family was. He started doing odd jobs around his neighborhood. Sometimes he painted portraits, and other times he fixed mechanical things which had broken. He soon realized that these odd jobs were not making enough money to support his family. He decided to move to Philadelphia to paint pictures. Philadelphia was even larger than Lancaster, and he hoped to paint many portraits. His plan worked. Before long, he had made enough money to buy a farm for his family.

In Philadelphia, he met Benjamin Franklin. Robert was already trying to build a boat powered by steam. He and Franklin had long talks about science. When Franklin told him about England and France, he decided to go to England to study art. In London, Fulton took lessons in painting from a famous artist named Benjamin West.

He also met scientists and inventors including James Watt who had invented the steam engine. Robert Fulton soon forgot all about his art as dreams of a steam-powered boat grew stronger. In 1793 he went to France to built a real steamboat. He launched his first try in the Seine River which runs through Paris. It sank.

"So you see, Billy, you're not alone," his father said.

"I guess I'm not," agreed Billy.

Anyway, Fulton didn't give up. Maybe it was because his boat sank that he worked next on steam submarines. I guess he thought he was already halfway there. He had already built a steam-powered boat that went under the water.

"Too bad you can't build a newspaper submarine," Mary said.

Billy frowned at his sister. Dad ignored Mary's joke and went on with his story.

The French were tired of boats that didn't work, so they sent him away. The English were interested in Fulton's ideas, though. They invited him to continue his work in England, and Robert gladly accepted. Not long after that he built a working submarine.

Robert Fulton missed his family. He decided to return to the United States to build his steamboat. Fulton moved back to America in 1806, and only a year later his invention was ready to test . He set August 11, 1807, as the date to launch his steamboat, called the "Clermont," in the Hudson River.

People crowded onto the New York City dock from which the Clermont would be launched. They lined the shores of the Hudson River. Most of the people who had come to watch thought the boat would sink. They didn't believe a boat could be powered by steam. As the Clermont cleared the dock, they had to change their minds. Fulton had succeeded. In fact, the steamboat floated and moved quickly all the way up the Hudson River to Albany.

Robert Fulton was a hero. Part of what made him a hero was that he didn't stop trying after his early failures.

"Now I think it's time for you to act like Robert Fulton," Dad said. "Remember, Fulton didn't invent the idea of the steamboat. He was just able to see how to make other people's ideas better. I showed you this morning how to make a sailboat out of newspaper. Now you need to try to figure out how to make that newspaper boat better."

"If I were really acting like Robert Fulton, I would put a steam engine in the boat," Billy joked.

"I doubt if a newspaper boat could be made strong enough to carry a steam engine. Perhaps, you'd better come up with other ideas."

"Well, I was thinking that if I made the bottom of the boat wider, it wouldn't fall over so much. Maybe I also could weight it a little to keep the wind from knocking it over.

His father congratulated him. "Those both sound like workable ideas."

Billy's new boat worked great. It even kept floating until they had to go back home!

Billy Anderson's Think Box

❏ Robert had two things he especially liked to do. Can you name them?

❏ How good was the first steamboat Robert Fulton built?

❏ Where did he go after the failure of his first steamboat?

○ Good thinking and trying new ideas helped Robert Fulton. Will taking the time to think about things carefully help you, too? What ideas would you like to try?

Sequoyah

Cherokee Alphabetizer

"I don't want to hear that story," Mary said. "I've heard it too many times already." Mary's brother, Billy, agreed. He had only suggested it because it was getting late. They were supposed to be picking a couple of books to hear before bedtime. They were having a hard time choosing, though. There were lots of books to choose from, but none of them seemed interesting. The children had heard them all before. Just then Grandpa George came into the room. "What's taking you kids so long?"

"We can't find a good story," Mary complained.

"They're all good stories, aren't they? You liked them before, anyway."

"That's the problem," Billy said. "We've already heard all of them. I bet you know stories we've never heard. What are books good for, anyway? Once you read them, you get bored with them."

"I can tell you what books are good for," Grandpa replied, "and it will be a story I bet you've never heard before. That will take care of all of your problems."

"Yeah!" both of the children cried at once. They loved Grandpa's stories.

We use books and writing mainly to remember things. A few books can hold more information than any one person. And remembering exactly what someone has said or thought is more important the more machines and science you have.

We didn't always have books and writing. A long time ago all the stories people wanted to hear had to be remembered. There were certain people whose job it was to remember stories. They would listen to the stories told by older people over and over again. Then, when they got older, it would be their turn to tell the stories. It's a little like the members of this family. I used to sit and listen to my father and grandfather tell stories. I heard them often so I still remember them. Now, I can tell the two of you these same stories.

However, writing and books are important. When I tell a story, only you two hear it. That's not many people. Even if I were to tell a story to all your friends, that still wouldn't be very many. A book is different. Many, many people can hear or read the story if it's written in a book. That means a lot more people can enjoy it and pass it on to their families and friends.

Now, this story is about an American Indian named Sequoyah.

"That's the name of a tree," Billy interrupted.

"That's right. Sequoyah was so important that some of the biggest and oldest trees are named after him," Grandpa said.

Sequoyah was a great man. He was a genius. He worked out a way to write down his Indian language. Sequoyah was a Cherokee Indian. When he was a boy, the Cherokees lived in the southeastern United States. Their lands were in the states of Georgia, Alabama, North Carolina, Tennessee, and Kentucky.

Even before the United States won its freedom from England, there were settlers who moved into the lands that belonged to the Indians. These settlers thought they had more right to the land. They had many reasons for thinking that. One reason was that the settlers thought of the Indians as savages. Another reason was that the Indians didn't seem to use the land very much. The settlers planned to use the land a lot. They cut down large parts of the forests so that they could plant large fields of crops.

What the settlers thought about the Indians wasn't true. The Indians were not savages. The settlers didn't understand the Indians because the Indian ways were different from those of the settlers. The Cherokees didn't plant large fields of crops. They did have vegetable gardens, though. The Indians didn't have large cities, but they did build villages of log cabins. They obtained much of their food by hunting and fishing.

One of the main reasons the settlers thought the Indians were savages was that the Indians didn't have a written language. Most people thought that a person had to have a written language to be civilized. Sequoyah decided that if he invented writing to go with the Cherokee language, he could save his people. If the settlers thought the Indians were civilized, maybe they would stop taking the lands of the Indians. The Cherokee language could have been written with our alphabet. But Sequoyah wanted to have a special alphabet just for the Cherokee language. That would show that it was like other languages.

"How do you go about inventing a written language?" Grandpa George asked.

Mary shook her head. "I don't know."

"Have you ever made up a code?" Grandpa asked.

"I have," said Billy proudly.

Grandfather looked at him. "How did you do it?"

"We traded every letter for a different one," Billy explained.

"So, you were still using an alphabet. Every letter stood for a few sounds. There are other ways to write a language," Grandpa said.

"Like what?" asked Mary.

"You could draw a picture for each word in the language," explained Grandpa.

Mary thought. "That would take a long time to write."

"Not only that, you would have a very large number of pictures to learn if you wanted to learn the language," Grandpa said. "And what about names? How do you write Mary or Billy? You have to draw a very good picture if you want to talk about a certain person."

"That would be too hard," Mary said.

"It would be very hard, but some people have done it. The Chinese language used to have a picture for every word," Grandpa said.

Drawing pictures was the first thing Sequoyah tried, but he soon decided that it was too hard. Then, he tried something else. It wasn't quite an alphabet. It was called a syllabary. Each letter stood for a syllable. I can explain what that is with the word "Cherokee." That word has three syllables. The first one sounds like "che," the second one is "ro," and the last one is "kee." In Sequoyah's system, Cherokee was spelled with only three letters. We use eight letters to spell the same word.

Sequoyah had invented his system to prove that the Cherokees were civilized. He had hoped to convince the settlers that the Indians should be allowed to keep their own lands. His plan didn't work. The settlers still wanted the lands of the Cherokees. The Indians were eventually moved to other lands which weren't as nice as their homelands. The new lands were ones that the settlers didn't want. Even though Sequoyah was a genius, the Indians still lost their homes.

"So you see that books and writing are important. Once, they almost saved the

Indians. Do you still think you have too many books?" Grandpa asked.

"Yes," Billy said, smiling. "As long as you have stories to tell us, why do we need books?" Mary giggled. The children climbed quickly off the couch.

"You little rascals," Grandpa said. The children laughed and ran upstairs to bed. Grandpa couldn't quite catch them. ✺

Grandpa George Anderson's Think Box

❏ Why did Sequoyah want to invent a written language for his people?

❏ Did he have a good idea?

❏ Why did the settlers take away the Indians' lands?

○ Take some time to think about how you would make a written language. Would you use many pictures instead of words, or would you make up your own letters to show sounds?

James Bridger

The Mountain Man

Grandpa George couldn't keep up with Mary and Billy as they ran into the house.

"How was your trip to the zoo?" asked their mother as they ran through the front door.

"It was great!" said Mary.

"Yeah," agreed Billy. "We were heroes."

"Heroes? What happened?"

"It started in the monkey house," Mary said. "The gorillas got loose."

"Everybody was screaming and running around," continued Billy. "One of the zoo people tried to get the gorillas back into their cage. One of the gorillas ran off and opened the lions' cage."

"And the tigers' cage, too," added Mary. "The lions and the tigers were running all over the place. The gorilla was so scared it got back into its cage."

"That's when we were heroes." Billy finished the story. "We threw our sandwiches into the lions' and tigers' cages. When they went in to eat them, the zoo people closed the doors and locked them in."

"Well, that's one way to get rid of the tuna sandwiches I packed for you," Mom commented.

"Did all of that really happen?" their father wanted to know.

"Sure it did," said Billy.

Mary nodded. "Just like we said."

"Well, maybe not just like that." Grandpa George was now standing behind the two children. Billy and Mary jumped because they hadn't heard him come in.

"That story did sound a bit tall," the children's father said, smiling.

"It was so tall it made that oak tree out front look like a potted plant," Grandpa George said.

"So that's what you kids were whispering and giggling about in the back seat. You were trying to get your stories straight."

"Why do you say our story was tall?" Mary asked.

"A tall tale is one that is full of exaggerations," their mother explained. "An exaggeration is when you make something sound more exciting or more dangerous or more anything than it really was."

"Some people have made quite a career out of telling tall tales," Grandpa said.

"Like you, Dad?" Dad looked at Grandpa with a twinkle in his eye.

"No, not like me," Grandpa chuckled. "I never made a penny from my tall tales. I could tell you the story of a great tall-tale teller if you'd like to hear it, though." Everyone wanted to hear the story. First they made Grandpa promise that he wouldn't exaggerate.

This is the story of James Bridger. He was one of the first people to see a lot of America's West. He became famous for how well he knew the western part of the United States. When large numbers of people started going out West, Jim was able to guide them. He knew the safest trails to take and the easiest passes through the mountains.

Jim also became well known for the stories he would tell. Whenever he guided a wagon train through the western United

States he would tell stories. He had plenty of stories to tell. Some of his stories were about adventures he had had. Some of his stories were about the wonders he had seen. Some of his stories were true, but others were just tall tales. Most people couldn't tell the true ones from the exaggerations. Some of the stories that sounded the wildest were about things he had really seen.

"But I'm telling this story out of order. We'd better start at the beginning," Grandpa interrupted himself.

Jim was born in 1804 in Virginia. When he was only eight years old his family moved to a farm near St. Louis in Missouri. The St. Louis area was still pretty wild at that time. Jim learned early how to live on the frontier.

Sadly, he also learned to live on his own early in life. Four years after the Bridger family moved to Missouri, Jim's mother died. A year later his father died as well. At the age of thirteen Jim was an orphan. He had to find a way to live.

Would either of you know what to do if you had to make your own way?

"No," said Billy with wide eyes. "I wouldn't know what to do."

"We can't work," said Mary. "We're too little."

"Well, folks on the frontier had to grow up quickly," Grandpa went on.

Jim got a job with a blacksmith. A blacksmith is a person who makes things out of iron, like horseshoes. Blacksmiths must be strong because they use large hammers to shape the iron.

Jim worked for the blacksmith for five years. He grew strong, but he wasn't happy. Being a blacksmith was not exciting enough for Jim.

When Jim was eighteen he decided to find something more fun to do. He joined a group of trappers who were going west to the Rocky Mountains. Their job was to collect beaver skins for the Rocky Mountain Fur Company. The furs would then be made into coats and hats. Beaver hats were very stylish at that time.

"You promised not to exaggerate, Grandpa," Mary scolded. "Nobody would wear beavers for hats."

"I haven't exaggerated yet," Grandpa replied. "When the beaver skins were made into hats, they didn't look like beavers anymore."

Jim liked trapping more than blacksmithing. He liked being out in the wilderness. Few people had been where he was going. Almost everything he and the other trappers saw was new to them. Of course, the Indians who lived in the area knew all about it. But since most Indians and settlers didn't get along, few people who weren't Indians had heard any stories about the western territories.

Jim Bridger and the group of trappers hunted along the Yellowstone River because there were many beavers in that area. None of the trappers knew where the river went. Jim decided to find out. He floated down the river in a little boat made out of the skin of a buffalo. At the end of the river there was a large body of water that tasted salty. Jim thought it was part of the Pacific Ocean.

He climbed up one of the high hills next to this body of water. He saw that it was not connected to the ocean. It was a lake. He went back and told his friends he had found a salty lake. They didn't believe him. They had already heard some of his other stories.

Later, the trappers all explored this salty body of water. It wasn't part of the ocean at all. They found out it was a lake just as Jim had told them. Jim had discovered the Great Salt Lake, which is in Utah. Most lakes are fresh water, not salt water. The Great Salt Lake is different. It's just like the ocean. That's why Jim was fooled at first. Later, when he told the settlers he was guiding westward about the Great Salt Lake, few believed him.

Many of Jim's stories seemed too strange to be true. He told stories about the Yellowstone area. One story was about a spring whose water was hot enough to cook a fish. He also told of geysers that shot boiling water seventy feet or more into the air. These stories, as strange as they sounded, were true. The wonders Jim described can be found in what is now Yellowstone National Park.

As I said, some of Jim's stories were true and some were not. One of his tall stories was about a time he was hunting for food for a group of trappers. Suddenly he saw an elk through the trees. He took careful aim and fired. The elk didn't react at all. It didn't even jump at the sound of his rifle. He crept closer and took another shot. Still the elk didn't move at all. Confused, Jim fired his gun twice more. The elk just kept on eating grass and leaves. Jim was usually a very good shot. He couldn't believe he had missed so many times. He got angry and rushed at the elk. He was going to try to just hit the animal with his gun. He ran right into a wall of glass. He said there was actually a mountain of glass between him and the elk.

"Jim told so many stories like this last one that people didn't believe him when he told the truth about the Yellowstone area. That's why you kids need to be careful when you tell stories that you've made up. People might get into the habit of not believing you."

"People still believe you, don't they?" Billy asked.

"Of course, they do," Grandpa answered. "Why shouldn't they? Don't you think my stories are true?"

"Well, there is that story about how you landed the airplane all by yourself when the pilot fainted," said Dad.

"And the one about how the Queen of England invited you to dinner," added Mom.

"And the one about the pirate and . . . "

"All right, all right," said Grandpa. "Maybe some of them are a little tall."

"They're so tall," Mary laughed, "they make the oak tree out front look like a potted plant!"

Everybody laughed. 🌾

Mary Anderson's Think Box

❏ What is a tall tale?

❏ When you make up a tall-tale story, do you always remember to tell your listeners it is not a true story? What could happen if you didn't?

❏ James Bridger discovered the Great Salt Lake. Did everyone believe him. Why?

○ Do you think you would know the difference between a true story and a tall tale? What clues would help you decide?

Davy Crockett
King of the Wild Frontier

"I'm in trouble, Uncle Bob," Billy said
quietly. "Can I talk to you?"

Uncle Bob was sitting by himself in the living
room reading the paper. He and Aunt Anne had
come over for Sunday dinner. Everyone else

was busy in the kitchen getting the meal ready.

"Of course, William," his uncle answered. "You can talk to me anytime."

"Can I talk to you alone?" Billy asked.

Uncle Bob laid aside his paper. "This must be serious. Come on, let's take a walk outside while they finish cooking."

They walked almost two blocks before Billy said anything. "Can I come live with you?" he finally asked.

"Why do you want to do that?" Uncle Bob looked surprised.

"I'm sure Dad won't want me to stay at home," Billy answered in a small voice.

"And I'm sure that you're wrong," said Uncle Bob. "Now tell me what this is all about."

"You know Dad's video camera?"

"Yes, Billy, I know it very well. Your father uses it all the time. Just about every time we get together he makes me wave at the camera. Did something happen to it?"

Billy nodded. "I wanted to show it to my friends. Dad told me not to play with it, but I took it outside yesterday. While I was showing it to Tommy, I accidentally dropped it. The lens part broke. Dad loves that camera, and now I've broken it."

"Your dad may love that camera," said Uncle Bob, "but he loves you more. He's not going to want you to go away."

They had reached the park. "Really?" asked Billy.

"Of course," Uncle Bob assured him. "You aren't the first person to think that you had to leave home because you had upset your parents. Let's sit on that bench over there. I'll tell you the story of a boy who ran away and then found out that he didn't have to."

This is the story of Davy Crockett. Davy was born in 1786 in Tennessee. At that time, Tennessee was still the frontier. Few Americans had gone there. For those who lived there, life was hard and dangerous.

Davy was a child of the frontier. He loved the adventure. He was even more wild than you are—though, the way your mom talks sometimes, she may not believe me.

One of Davy's earliest memories was of an adventure he almost had. At the time, he was probably younger than you are. Davy's four older brothers and an older friend were in a canoe. The older boys had left Davy on the riverbank. A little ways downriver, the canoe started drifting toward a waterfall. The Crockett boys knew all about handling canoes. However, their older friend didn't, and he was the one holding the paddle. He was too afraid to give the paddle to any of the Crockett brothers, and he couldn't use it himself. The canoe edged closer and closer to the waterfall. Finally, a man working in a nearby field saw that the boys were in danger. He dived into the river and pulled the canoe to safety.

"Davy had seen everything from the riverbank. He was very upset. Do you know why?" Uncle Bob asked Billy.

"Was it because his brothers could have drowned?"

"Well, that's what you might think, but that's not why Davy Crockett was so upset. He was very angry about missing out on all of the excitement. Even though everybody in the canoe might have died, he wished he had been in on the adventure. Davy was that kind of boy.

"But that's the wrong story. I was going to tell you what happened when Davy ran away from home."

Davy Crockett had many adventures as a young man. He also worked hard. There was plenty to do on frontier farms. Many people on the frontier thought farm work was more important than school work. Davy was about your age before he went to school at all.

When he was thirteen, Davy's parents decided he should learn how to read and write. He had been in school for only four days when he got into a fight with another boy. Davy was afraid to go back to school. He knew that the schoolmaster would punish him. For the next few days, instead of going to school he spent the time in the woods.

When Davy didn't show up at school for several days, the schoolmaster sent a note to his parents asking if Davy was all right. Then,

Mr. Crockett knew Davy was playing instead of going to school. He knew Davy needed to learn to read and write if he was to be successful in life. So Mr. Crockett threatened Davy with even more punishment than he would get from the schoolmaster for fighting. Davy felt trapped between two punishments. He also felt that he had disappointed his father. Davy ran away.

He knew of a man who was preparing to drive a herd of cattle from Tennessee to Virginia. Davy signed on to help drive the cattle. It took many weeks to walk the cattle over the mountains and through the valleys to Virginia. Davy had planned to return to Tennessee with the man that owned the cattle, but they got separated in Virginia. Davy had to find his own way home.

Davy took two years to get back to Tennessee from Virginia. He had many interesting experiences along the way. Several times he had to stop and get a job so he could buy food.

When he reached home, he learned that his father was operating a kind of inn. He didn't know if his family would want to see him again. He remembered how angry his father had been with him right before he left. Now, he had been gone a long time. Would they want him back?

Davy knew he had changed a lot in the two years he had been gone. He had grown up. When he left, he had been thirteen. Now, he was fifteen. He decided not to tell anyone who he was until he could find out how his family felt about him. Davy went into his father's inn and asked for a room for the night. No one had recognized him yet.

A little later, everyone who was staying in the inn that night gathered for dinner. Halfway through the meal, his oldest sister suddenly recognized him. She ran to him and hugged him around the neck. "Here is my lost brother!"

Davy was quickly surrounded by his whole family. Everyone wanted to hug him, shake his hand, and pat him on the back. They were all glad to see him. He had been gone so long they thought he had died.

Then Davy was ashamed of himself. He was sorry he had caused his family so much pain. They loved him, and they had worried about him for the two years he had been away.

Davy Crockett later became a famous hunter and trapper. People said that he was the "best bear hunter there ever was." He made friends with another famous man from Tennessee. That was Andrew Jackson, our seventh president. Davy died in 1836 fighting to free Texas from Mexico. All through his exciting life he never forgot the lesson he had learned as a young man: No matter what he did, he could always count on the love of his family.

"You think that's how Mom and Dad are going to feel about me?" Billy asked.

"I'm sure of it," Uncle Bob said with a smile. "Now we'd better be getting on back for dinner. After we eat, you and I can talk to your father about that camera."

Uncle Bob Anderson's Think Box

❏ What words can you use to describe Davy Crockett?

❏ When did his parents decide he should go to school?

❏ What mistakes did Davy make that caused his family to feel sad?

○ Is it ever good to run away from your problems? Can it often make them worse? How do you treat the members of your family? Do you show them that you love them by what you say and do?

Sam Houston

The Raven

"**G**o home! I don't want to play with you anymore!" Billy shouted from the porch.

His mother was inside reading. She heard him shouting. "William, come in here at once!" she called.

"Yes, Mom." He came inside slowly. Whenever his mother called him William, he was in trouble.

"Who were you yelling at?"

"Paul," answered Billy in a small voice.

"I thought so. Why can't you two play nicely together?"

"He always has to take over the game," Billy complained. "He makes his own rules, and everybody has to play his way."

"Have you tried to get along with him?" Billy's mother asked.

"Yes, I have tried and tried, like you said. It's no use. We're like cowboys and Indians."

"What do you mean?"

"We can never get along," Billy answered. "Just like cowboys and Indians, we can never be friends."

"Well, dear, I'd like you to keep trying. You know, sometimes even cowboys and Indians can be friends. Maybe it would help if I told you a story about a cowboy who was a good friend of the Indians. What do you think?"

"That might help," Billy said. This was turning out better than he thought it would. Instead of being punished, he was going to hear a story.

"Many cowboys have come from Texas," Billy's mother began. "I'll tell you the story of one of the great Texans, a cowboy. He made Texas what it is today. This man was also a great friend of the Indians."

This is the story of Sam Houston. Sam was born in 1793, but not in Texas. He was born in Virginia. When he was about thirteen, his family moved to Tennessee. At that time Tennessee was a dangerous frontier area. The Houston family lived just east of the Tennessee River. The west side of the river was Indian country. The Cherokee Indians lived there.

When the Houston family arrived in Tennessee, there was nothing there. Their land was mostly woods. Sam and his five older brothers built the log cabin that would be their home. Then they cleared another place in the forest so they could plant vegetables.

His brothers soon found out that Sam was useless on a farm. He hated farm work and got out of it whenever he could. Although Sam had not been a good student in Virginia, now he read whenever and whatever he could. His brothers decided Sam would be of more use to the family with another kind of job. He found work as a clerk in the village store. His paycheck helped the family.

But Sam was no happier as a clerk than he had been on the farm. One day, when he was fifteen years old, he packed a few of his things and left the village. He didn't forget to take a few of his favorite books. His destination surprised everyone. He crossed to the west side of the Tennessee River, into Indian Country, to live with the Indians.

Sam was happy with the Cherokee Indians. They treated him like a friend, and he learned many things from them. The first thing he learned was the Cherokee language. He had many chances to use it throughout his life. After Sam had learned their language, the Cherokees were able to teach him all they knew about living in the forest. He learned to hunt and fish as they did. He also learned many secrets of the natural world.

The Cherokees liked Sam so much they made him a part of their tribe. The chief, Oo-loo-te-ka, treated him like his own son. The Indians even gave Sam an Indian name. They called him *Co·lon·neh* which means "The Raven." Ravens were important to the Cherokees, so this was a special name.

Sam lived with the Cherokees for three years, but he never forgot that he was an American. When the United States went to war with England, he left the Indians and joined the army. He fought under General Andrew Jackson during the War of 1812. Jackson later became our seventh president. Sam fought against another tribe of Indians, the Creeks, who were helping the English soldiers against the Americans. Sam was very brave in the war and earned the respect of General Jackson.

After the war, Sam went back to visit the Cherokees. This time he had a job to do. It had become well known that Sam knew the

Cherokee language and that the Indians liked him. That was why the government chose him to solve some problems between the United States and the Cherokee tribe. Sam did his best to be fair to his old friends and to his government.

By the time he had finished his mission to the Indians, he knew what he wanted to be. He decided to study law so that he could become a politician. He thought that as a member of the government he could work to protect his Cherokee friends. In 1822, Sam was elected to the House of Representatives three times. Then in 1827, he became the governor of Tennessee. However, not everyone liked this friend of the Indians. After only two years as governor, he was forced to leave Tennessee.

It was not a surprise that when he was in trouble Sam went back to his old friends, the Indians. The Cherokee tribe was no longer living in Tennessee. That state was filling up with settlers. The Indians had been moved to new homes west of the Mississippi River. Few settlers had crossed the Mississippi yet. The Indians had these new lands almost all to themselves. Sam helped the Cherokees set up new homes. His brothers may have found this funny. Sam had not been much help when the Houston family was setting up its new home in Tennessee. Now he was helping the Indians do it! His Cherokee friends were happy to see him and for the help he could give.

Part of the help he gave his friends was to speak for them in Washington, D.C. Sam felt the Indians were being cheated. Lands that the United States government gave the Indians were later taken away. The government was unable to stop settlers from taking other Indian lands. In 1832, Sam went to Washington, D.C., to speak to the president. By that time Sam's friend, Andrew Jackson, was president. Jackson didn't help the Cherokees. Instead, he asked Sam to help the government make agreements with other Indian tribes in Texas. Sam agreed to work for the American government again.

When Sam got to Texas, it was still part of Mexico. Sam started helping the people to win their freedom. Three years later, in 1835, war between Texas and Mexico began. The Texans chose Sam as their leader. The war did not last long. You may have already guessed that the Texans won because Texas is now part of the United Sates. Sam won a great victory in April of 1836 on the San Jacinto River.

Texas was free from Mexico, but it didn't become a state right away. For a while it was an independent country. Texas is the only U.S. state that has also been a country. Sam Houston was elected as the first president of the country of Texas. A few years later, when Texas became a state, Sam was elected as its first governor. The Texans liked him so much they named a large city after him.

"You mean there's a city named Sam?" Billy laughed.

"No, silly," his mother answered. "You know that they named the city Houston."

"Yeah," said Billy. "I know."

"So you see, dear, even cowboys and Indians can get along just fine. Anybody can be friends. It just takes wanting to."

"But I don't want to be Paul's friend." said Billy.

"But I want you to," said his mother with a smile. "And that is what counts." ✺

Billy Anderson's Think Box

❏ Sam did not like farm work. His brothers decided he should do something else to help provide money for the family. What did he try next? Did he like it?

❏ When Sam went to live with the Indians they gave him a new name. What was it and what did it mean?

❏ How did Sam help the Indians after the war?

○ It is good to be kind to all different kinds of people. Jesus loves all the children in the world. Can you think of ways to be a helpful friend to everyone you know?

Samuel F. B. Morse

Writing in Code

"What's that supposed to be?" Billy asked.

"It's a painting of the big tree in our front yard," Mary answered. "And that's Queenie, the yellow cat from next door, sitting on one of the branches."

"It doesn't look like our tree. It looks like a tall brown man with a yellow face and green hair."

Mary frowned. "It does not. It looks like what it's supposed to be. Besides, I'm just practicing. I'm going to be a great artist when I grow up."

"Not unless you can do better than that," Billy laughed. "Anyway, yesterday you were going to be a doctor. Can't you make up your mind?"

Mary picked up one of her paint brushes to throw at Billy. He dodged and bumped into their mother who was coming into the room.

"Be nice to your sister, please, Billy," Mom said.

"She's the one throwing things," Billy said.

"I heard you teasing her. That's not very nice."

"But now she's going to be an artist. Yesterday, she was going to be a doctor. It's silly to keep changing your mind like that." Billy tried to explain why it was okay to make fun of Mary.

"And how many things have you wanted to be?" his mother asked him.

"I don't know." Billy could see he had lost this argument.

"Some important people have had trouble deciding what they wanted to be," their mother explained. "Sometimes the things for which they are famous are not the first things they wanted to be."

Mary was glad to hear that. She had begun to think that maybe it was wrong to keep changing her mind. "Can you tell us a story about someone like that?"

"Certainly," Mom said. "I'll tell you the story of Samuel Morse. He invented a code and a way to get a message quickly to someone far away. However, that wasn't what he wanted to do first. Before he was an inventor, he was a good artist.

Samuel Morse was born in 1791 in Charlestown, Massachusetts. His father was a preacher, and he had many brothers and sisters. Even when he was still a boy, he was curious and had a lot of energy. He split his time between science and art. Samuel loved both of these subjects.

As a young man, he went to Yale College. There he heard about electricity. This was a long time ago, almost 200 years ago. People didn't know much about electricity at that time. Samuel found it quite interesting. He learned as much as he could about electricity.

When he was older, it would be his work with electricity that would make him famous. Of course, he didn't know that. When he finished college, he did not choose to study more about it. Even though he was interested in science, it was art he loved. Samuel wanted to be an artist. After college, he went to London to study painting.

Morse became a very good artist. He found that his favorite subject was scenes from the past. He painted large pictures of historical events or people. This kind of painting was popular at the time in Europe. Samuel Morse, the artist, became well known.

Not long after he finished studying art, he came back to the United States. Many people here already knew about him and how good an artist he was. However, his historical paintings were not as popular in America as they were in Europe. Samuel wasn't able to earn enough selling these paintings. To make more money, he started painting portraits. Many people wanted a painting of themselves, or someone they loved, to hang on their walls.

"In fact, that is still a popular kind of art. That's why we have pictures of you two and the rest of our family in the living room," Mom said.

"Too many pictures of other people, I think," Mary said, "and not enough pictures of us." She sat up straight, smoothed down her hair, and smiled prettily as if she were having her picture taken.

"We don't need any more pictures of you, that's for sure," Billy said. Mary picked up another paint brush to throw at him, but her mother stopped her.

"That's enough of that," she said. "Do you want to hear the rest of the story?"

"Yes, Mom," the children said.

"All right, then," Mom continued.

When Samuel Morse started painting portraits, he found that many people wanted their pictures painted by him. He went to Charleston, South Carolina, and received 150 requests for portraits in just a few weeks.

Even with all of these paintings to paint, Samuel still had a hard time getting by. Also, he didn't like painting portraits as much as he had liked painting big historical scenes. He went back to Europe so he could paint his big history paintings. This time he didn't do well there. On the boat ride back to the United States, he began to worry. What could he do to support himself?

On the boat, he met a man named Dr. Charles Jackson. Dr. Jackson was an expert on electricity. Samuel Morse remembered how interested he had been in electricity in college. He was amazed at what had been discovered since then. Morse and Jackson had many long discussions on the boat from Europe to America. They talked about many ways that electricity could be used to make people's lives better. Samuel Morse was interested in trying to build a machine through which people could communicate over long distances. As soon as he arrived in the United Sates, he began working on this project.

Morse had to invent two things. First, he had to work out a code so that each letter of our alphabet could be sent through his machine. He developed a system of short and long taps. Each letter is a combination of shorts and longs. This is called Morse code.

The second part of his invention was a way to send Morse code over long distances through electric wires. Someone tapped the code for the letters at one end of the wire. Another person at the other end of the wire heard the taps and changed them back into letters. This part of Morse's invention was called the telegraph. Telegraph is a word made of two Greek words. *Tele* means "far away" and *graph* means "writing." So a telegraph is a way of writing a message from far away.

It took some time for people to understand the importance of the telegraph. Morse had to show his invention to Congress three times before they would give him enough money to build a real telegraph. In 1840, he connected Baltimore, Maryland, to Washington, D.C., with a telegraph wire. These cities are more than twenty miles apart. The old way to get news from one town to the other was by train. A message could be sent much faster by telegraph than by the train. When people saw this, they became interested in Morse's invention. Soon, telegraph wires connected cities all over the country.

"So you see," Mom told Billy and Mary, "the thing you do first is not necessarily the thing you will do best. Few people now remember that Samuel Morse was a fine painter. They usually think of him as the inventer of the telegraph and Morse code. There's nothing wrong with changing your mind about what is interesting to you or what you want to do."

"Thanks, Mom," Billy said. "That was a good story."

"I'm glad you liked it," his mother replied. "What did you think of the story, Mary?"

"I liked it." Mary was busy packing up her paints and brushes.

"What are you doing? Aren't you going to practice painting?" Mary's mother asked her.

"No, I've changed my mind," Mary said. "I don't want to be a painter anymore. I'm going to be an inventor."

"Oh, boy!" Billy said. "You'd better not tell her any more stories or she'll change her mind again." They all laughed as Billy dodged another paint brush. ❧

Katherine Anderson's Think Box

❏ What were Samuel's favorite subjects?

❏ What kind of paintings did Samuel like to paint best? He was a good artist. Did he earn enough money for his paintings to support himself?

❏ What did Samuel Morse invent?

○ Is it okay to change your mind about what you want to be when you grow up? Is it possible to do more than one thing sometimes? What would you like to do when you have finished getting an education?

Maria Mitchell

Stargazer

Mary came in from the front porch. "Do we have a telescope, Daddy?" she asked.

"I'm sorry, dear. We don't. Why do you ask?"

"I want to study the moon and the stars," Mary replied. "I have a lot of questions."

"What kind of questions, dear?" her mother asked.

Daddy smiled. "Now you've done it. You shouldn't have asked her that. She'll have so many questions, we'll never get her to bed."

Mary grinned at her father's joke but listed her questions anyway. "How far away is the moon? How big is it? How many stars are there? Why do they make patterns? Are some stars brighter because they are bigger or because they are closer? How far away are they?"

"Enough, enough," said Mary's father. "I told you there would be too many questions."

"I don't think you could find the answers to all of those questions even if we did have a telescope, dear," her mother added. "Even astronomers don't know the answers to all of those questions. Astronomers are scientists who study the stars, and they haven't discovered how many stars there are."

"Besides," said Billy, "you're too young to be an astronomer."

"That may not be true," her mother said. "One of the first women who was a scientist in America was an astronomer. She started very young. Her name was Maria Mitchell. Would you like to hear about her?"

"Yes, please, Mom." Mary smiled at her brother. "I want to hear about the young girl astronomer."

Maria Mitchell was born a long time ago, in the year 1818. The Mitchell family lived on Nantucket Island which is close to Massachusetts. Maria's father had many jobs on the island. He made watches, sold insurance, and did several other things. His most important job was being the island's astronomer.

Now, you may not think that being an astronomer is an important job. But in those days, it was. Most of the people on Nantucket Island were whalers. That means they hunted whales. Many things could be made from the parts of a whale. Whaling was very important in New England at that time.

When the boats were so far out to sea that the whalers couldn't see the land, they needed another way to tell where they were. The whalers did it by looking at the stars. They had instruments with which they could measure exactly where the stars were in the sky.

That wasn't all they needed to know, however. You know that the stars move through the sky at night. So measuring the position of the stars wasn't enough. The whalers also had to know exactly what time it was when they measured the stars. Knowing those two things, a whaler could figure out exactly where he was on the wide open sea. Making sure the clocks on board the whaling ships were accurate was the job of the astronomer. The clocks would be timed with the movements of the stars. Without Mr. Mitchell's careful work with their clocks, the whalers might be lost at sea. Everyone on Nantucket Island depended on Mr. Mitchell.

Even when Maria was still quite young, her father taught her about the stars. Whenever the weather was clear, she and her father would sit for hours and watch the stars through his telescope. It didn't matter if it was the middle of winter. Maria and her father bundled up in their warm clothes and climbed up on the roof to use the telescope.

Maria learned quickly. The people of Nantucket Island would say, "That Maria Mitchell certainly is clever, for a girl. Her father has taught her some good tricks." Soon they would learn that Maria's skill with a telescope was not just a trick.

One summer when Maria was about twelve years old, a whaling captain came to her house. "How do you do, Mrs. Mitchell?" he said to Maria's mother. "We sail tomorrow. I need to have your husband check my clock before we leave."

"I'm sorry, Captain," said Mrs. Mitchell. "Mr. Mitchell is on the other side of the island on business. I don't know what we can do."

"Mother," said Maria, "let me check the captain's clock. You know I have helped Father many times. I can do it."

The captain of the whaling ship didn't like the idea, but there was nothing he could do. He had to have his clock set just right, or he might get lost at sea. He left the clock with Maria Mitchell.

That night, before she went to bed, Maria studied the stars and the captain's clock. The clock was a little off, so she adjusted it. The next day she gave it back to the captain. He still looked unhappy. He wasn't sure if he could trust the little girl to have set his clock accurately. He checked it that night with the stars. He pretended not to know where he was and used the stars and the clock to tell him. They said he was in the harbor of Nantucket Island. The clock was right! He sent a member of his crew to the Mitchell house to thank Maria.

News soon spread that Maria was becoming as good an astronomer as her father. Some people had a hard time believing that a girl could be a scientist. However, now they had to believe it. A few years later, Maria had a chance to prove to the whole world what she had proven to the people of Nantucket Island.

As Maria got older, she held several jobs. When she was sixteen, she opened a school. Later, she became a librarian. But her first love was always astronomy. She began to feel that the stars were her personal friends. She knew many of them by name, and she talked to them at night while using her telescope.

Then, Maria heard about an astronomy contest. King Frederick the Sixth of Denmark was offering a gold medal to the first person to spot a new comet. A comet is like a shooting star, but it stays in the sky for weeks or months. Maria was sure that if she won the prize, people would know she was a serious scientist.

On October 1, 1847, she spotted a comet. But her letter to King Frederick couldn't leave Nantucket Island right away because of bad weather. While Maria's letter waited on board the mail ship in Nantucket Harbor, other scientists spotted the comet. No one was sure if King Frederick would believe Maria Mitchell had been the first to find the comet. One year later, in October of 1848, Maria received her answer. A package arrived for her from the King of Denmark. It contained the gold medal with Maria's name carved on it. Now, she thought, everyone would see her as a real scientist. However, not everyone did.

That same year, it was suggested that Maria be made a member of the American Academy of Arts and Sciences. There were no women members at that time. Some of the scientists in that group didn't want her to join.

"A woman scientist?" they said. "There can be no such thing. Women are not smart enough to be scientists. This must be some kind of trick. This Maria Mitchell can't have really found that comet."

Luckily, there were other scientists who felt that Maria belonged in their group. "What does it matter if she is a man or a woman?" they asked. "Science is science. Anyone who can use science to find the truth should be here with us."

Maria's supporters won the argument. Maria Mitchell became the first woman to be a member of the American Academy of Arts and Sciences. Two years later she became the first woman member of the American Association for the Advancement of Science. This time there was no argument. Maria Mitchell had proven that women could be scientists.

After the American Civil War, Matthew Vassar hired her to teach at his new college. Not everyone liked the idea of women attending college. For a woman to teach at a college was even harder for some people to accept. But Maria did it and did it well. Throughout her teaching, though, she always made time to keep studying the stars and making discoveries.

"So you see, dear," Mom said, "it's never too early to start being an astronomer."

"But we still don't have a telescope," Mary complained.

"There are a lot of stars you can see without a telescope. We can start with those. I can teach you the names of some of them if you'd like."

"That's great!" Mary was smiling again.

As Mary and her mother were going out onto the porch, Billy asked, "Can I come, too?"

"Sure," said Mary. "I guess boys can be astronomers, too."

Mary Anderson's Think Box

❑ What is an astronomer?

❑ What did Maria learn from her father?

❑ How was she able to help a whaling captain, when she was twelve years old?

❑ Was Maria a good scientist? Why do you think so?

○ It is fun to learn about new things. Asking questions is one way to learn. What other ways can you learn about things that interest you?

Elizabeth Blackwell
America's First Woman Doctor

"That's silly," said Susan. "Girls aren't doctors. Girls are nurses, and boys are doctors."

Mary objected, "Girls can be whatever they want. They can be doctors. Who told you they couldn't?"

"My daddy told me," Susan said.

"Let's go ask him."

The two girls ran downstairs. They found Susan's father in the living room watching television. "That's right," he said when the girls asked him their question. "Women aren't supposed to be doctors. They make much better nurses. That's because being a nurse is like being a mommy. Nurses put on bandages and make people feel better."

The two girls went back upstairs. Mary was a little confused and a little sad. "I don't think that's right," she told Susan. "That's not what my mommy said. I'm going to ask her again."

When she got home, Mary asked her mother the same question she had asked Susan's father. "Of course girls can be whatever they want to be," Mary's mother said. "There are many women who are doctors and many men who are nurses. It wasn't always like that, though. Once, almost everyone thought the way Susan's father thinks. We know better now because of one woman. Her name was Elizabeth Blackwell. She was brave enough to go to medical school and become a doctor when most people thought it was wrong for a woman to do that. Would you like to hear her story?"

Elizabeth Blackwell was born in 1821 in England. Her father was a successful business man, but he didn't think the way most people did at that time. Mr. Blackwell had other ideas about what was right and what was wrong. He thought it was wrong for children eight or ten years old to work in factories. Most other people thought this was all right.

"What do you think, dear? Would you like to work in a factory for ten or twelve hours a day?"

Mary wrinkled her face with a frown. "No, thank you. I'm sure I'm too young for that."

"Well, it's lucky for you that ideas about children working have changed. Otherwise, we might have to send you off to work. Maybe we should think about it anyway."

"No, don't," Mary giggled.

Mary's mother continued her story.

Many people owned slaves at that time. Mr. Blackwell thought slavery was wrong. He also thought that little girls should receive the same education as little boys. This was very different thinking for his time. Most people didn't think girls were as smart as boys; it was a waste of time to try to teach girls. After all, girls only needed to know how to do housework. That was the only job that women could have. Happily, most people know now that boys aren't smarter than girls. They can each do the same jobs.

People started to dislike Mr. Blackwell and his family because he had these new ideas. Finally, he had to move from England to the United States. That was in 1832 when Elizabeth was eleven years old. He hoped to find other people in America who had the same ideas he did. Unfortunately, most people here didn't like Mr. Blackwell's ideas either. When the Blackwell family moved to the United States, it was still legal in some places for white people to own black people. The one thing that Mr. Blackwell was able to do was to educate his daughters the same way he did his sons.

Elizabeth became well educated. She easily got a teaching job when she was eighteen. Her new job was in Kentucky where slavery was still legal. Elizabeth often spoke out against slavery. To her, it was a great evil. The people who had given her the job didn't like the fact that she taught her students that slavery was wrong. She was not able to keep her job long.

Instead of looking for another teaching job right away, she decided to help a friend who was very ill. Elizabeth cooked and cleaned and sat with her friend all day. Her friend was dying of cancer and sometimes she was in great pain.

On one very bad day, her friend cried out, "Oh, if only there had been a woman doctor for me to talk to, maybe I would not feel so bad now."

Mary knew what her friend meant. At that time, people didn't talk to each other about private matters. They were too embarrassed. Elizabeth's friend, like many women, had not felt comfortable speaking about her health with a male doctor. If the doctor had been a woman, she might have been more comfortable talking to her. The doctor might have found out what was wrong with Elizabeth's friend in time to cure it.

Unfortunately, there were no women doctors. Medicine was thought to be a man's job. Women were not allowed to go to medical school. Mary decided right then and there that she would become the first woman doctor. All of her friends tried to tell her this was a foolish idea. "There are no women doctors, and there never will be. Even though you would be a good doctor, you'll never get a chance to prove it. No medical school will let you in."

Mary did not change her mind. She was determined! Before she could get into a medical school she would have to earn the money to pay for the classes. She would also have to know something about medicine. She got another teaching job where she would have access to a library of medical books. After six years, she had enough money to go to college. Then, her real work began. She had to find a school that would let her in.

Elizabeth wrote letters to almost every medical school in the country. She started with the larger schools and then wrote to the smaller ones. Every place she wrote sent back letters refusing to let her study at that school. Some of these letters were nice, but most were rude.

Finally, Elizabeth wrote the Geneva Medical College in New York State. The teachers at that school didn't want her any more than the teachers at the other colleges. "I have never heard of such a thing," one of the teachers said. "A woman at a medical college; it's impossible."

"She can't be serious," another teacher said.

"Why don't we let the students vote on this?" suggested the president of the college. "They are sure to feel the same way we do. They will never allow a woman to join them at this school; but when they refuse her, we will not be blamed for being old-fashioned."

The other teachers liked his idea. Fortunately, their plan backfired. As a joke, the students voted to allow Elizabeth Blackwell to attend Geneva Medical College. Everyone was surprised when she arrived ready for school in the fall of 1847. It took a while, but Elizabeth showed everyone that she was a good student. Two years later, in 1849, Dr. Elizabeth Blackwell became the first woman doctor in the United States.

However, though Elizabeth now qualified as a doctor, her fight was not over. People had never heard of a woman doctor. They didn't trust her. They thought she could not be as good as a male doctor. It was years before she was able to attract enough patients to open a clinic.

In 1866, Dr. Elizabeth Blackwell opened her own medical school, the New York Women's Medical College. The course at Dr. Blackwell's school was much more complete than the one she had taken at Geneva. Students had to be in school for four years to graduate from the New York Women's Medical College. Only two years had been required at Geneva. The graduates of Dr. Blackwell's school learned more about medicine before they started seeing patients. Because of that, they were probably better doctors. Since that time, there have been thousands of women doctors. They have proven women can be great doctors.

"Thank you for the story, Mommy," Mary said. "I feel better now." She got up and put on her coat.

"You're welcome, dear. Where are you going?"

"I'm going to go tell Susan that story. I want her to feel better, too." ❧

Susan's Think Box

❑ Elizabeth's father thought differently about some things. What were they?

❑ What made Elizabeth think about becoming a doctor? Were there many women doctors in that time?

❑ What did Elizabeth do to make it easier for other women to become doctors?

○ Do women make good doctors? Do men make good nurses? God gives each person talents. What are your special talents?

Frederick Douglass
From Bondage to Freedom

“When will Mom and Dad be home
again?” Billy asked his grandfather.
Billy had been staring out the window. He was
looking up and down the street hoping to see
his parents drive up in their car. The rain kept
him and his sister, Mary, inside. It also kept

him from getting a good look at the passing cars until they were right in front of the house.

Grandma Brigit and Grandpa David had been staying with the children while their parents were away. Grandpa put down the newspaper he had been reading. "I keep telling you the same thing," he said. "Their plane lands at 5:00, so they won't be here until dinner time."

"They've been gone a long time," said Mary. She was sitting in the middle of the living room floor. There were coloring books and crayons and dolls and other toys all around her. She wasn't playing with any of them.

"I know it seems like a long time," her grandfather said, "but really, it's only been a week."

"They will come back, won't they?" She looked up at her grandfather, and he could tell she was sad.

"Of course they will, my dear. Why, they're almost home now," he answered. "Is that what you kids have been worried about?"

"I don't know," Mary said. She looked down at her pile of toys but didn't touch any of them.

"Come up here and sit by me," Grandpa David said. "You too, Billy. Come over here, and let's talk about this."

The children sat on the couch on either side of their grandfather. Mary moved in close so Grandpa could put his arm around her.

"Now, you mustn't worry," Grandpa said. He

hugged Mary and patted Billy on the knee. "Your parents miss you just as much as you miss them. Their trip is almost over, and I'm sure they can't wait to be with you again. And I've told you that they'll be home soon." He looked closely at his two grandchildren. Their sad expressions hadn't changed. Then he had another idea how to cheer up the children.

"You know," he said, "kids these days have it much better than kids used to." This was something Grandpa said all the time, and it usually got a smile. But not this time.

"Oh, Grandpa," Billy said. He was still trying to look out the window even though he was on the other side of the room now.

"Your grandfather used to tell your mother that all the time when she was a girl," said Grandma Brigit.

"This time I'm serious," their grandfather said. "Your parents can be with you whenever they want. No one can take you away from them, and no one can take them away from you. It wasn't always like that."

"Really?" asked Mary. Her eyes had gotten very large and round.

"That's right," Grandpa David answered. "Remember when we've talked about slavery before? Slaves weren't able to decide things like that. They couldn't choose to live with their families. If their master wanted to keep the parents and send the children away, he or she could just do it."

"That's bad," said Billy, turning away from the window.

"It was very bad," agreed his grandfather. "I know a story about a slave who was separated from his mother. When he grew up, he helped make it so this couldn't happen to anyone else. Would you like to hear the story?"

"Yes, please," both children said.

This is the story of Frederick Douglass. Frederick's mother was a slave; and when he was born, he was a slave too. His mother's name was Harriet Bailey. She named him Frederick Augustus Washington Bailey. Later, I'll tell you how he came to change his name.

He was born in 1817 in Maryland. People didn't keep good records about the lives of slaves, so he was never quite sure when his birthday was. He figured it was somewhere near St. Valentine's Day. That's on February 14th.

When little Frederick was only a week old, his mother was sent back to work in the fields. His grandmother, Betsey, took care of him. Frederick almost never got to see his mother. The fields she worked in were far away. She lived on a different part of the plantation, which is a very large type of farm.

Frederick missed his mother very much. Still, he was happy living with his grandmother. She was a kind woman and looked after him as if he were her own son.

However, his happiness didn't last long. When he was eight years old, he was sent to live in the master's house. Now he wasn't able to live with anyone in his family.

"Why did people treat slaves like that, Grandpa?" Mary wanted to know.

"Many slave owners didn't care enough about their slaves to worry about keeping their families together," he answered. "In fact, some slave owners broke up slave families on purpose. They thought the slaves would work better if they were sad."

"That doesn't make any sense." Mary frowned. "I can't do anything but cry when I'm sad."

At the main house, Frederick lived with some other slave children. The cook, who was also a slave, watched over them. Frederick didn't like the cook at all. She spanked him often, especially when he cried.

Frederick didn't have to stay with the cook long. A year after he started living in the main house, he was sent to another plantation. He wasn't sorry to leave the cook, but it did make him sad to be even farther from his mother. In fact, he never saw her again.

The wife of his new master, Mrs. Auld, was a kind woman. She taught him to read. That was fine until his master found out. His master was very angry with Mrs. Auld. "Never teach a slave to read," he said. "A slave who can read won't want to stay a slave."

Mr. Auld was right. Frederick had already decided to run away. To be able to get away from his master and out of the South altogether, he would have to pretend to be free. All free blacks in the South had to carry papers proving they were free. Frederick carried the papers of one of his friends. Disguised as a sailor, he rode the train north to New York State where there were no slaves. On the train, the police checked his papers. They didn't suspect a thing. His plan worked. Finally, at the age of eighteen, Frederick was free.

However, there were laws at that time which said that runaway slaves should be sent back to their masters. Most runaway slaves kept very quiet so they wouldn't be caught. But Frederick couldn't stay quiet for long. He did change his name from Frederick Bailey to Frederick Douglass and hoped no one would find out who he really was. Soon he started working with a group of abolitionists. Abolitionists were people who tried to end slavery. He even wrote his own life story to show people how bad slavery was. It was called *Narrative of the Life of Frederick Douglass*. That's how the slave hunters found him. Just before they were about to catch him, he managed to sail away to England. He wasn't able to come home until two years later. By that time, some of his friends had been able to buy his freedom from his old master. When he got back from England he wrote another story of his time as a slave and his escape. That book was called *My Bondage and My Freedom*. Before, Frederick had been free, but he had had to live in hiding. Now, there was no more need to hide. He could never be taken back to his old master.

Frederick Douglass made quite an impression on the people he met. He was good looking, intelligent, and spoke well. He met many important people, even presidents. He convinced people how evil slavery was, but he couldn't end slavery alone. In the end, it took a war to end slavery. During the Civil War, President Abraham Lincoln signed the Emancipation Proclamation. It freed the slaves in all of the rebelling states. Strangely enough, it did not free the slaves in Frederick's home state. Maryland was not a rebel state. Three of Frederick's sons fought in the Civil War. They fought to make freedom possible, and they won.

"So, you see how much luckier you are than Frederick was?" their grandfather asked them.

Just then a car pulled up in the driveway. "Mom and Dad are home! Mom and Dad are home!" yelled Mary as she ran to the door.

"Yay!" shouted Billy, right behind her.

When her mother came through the door, Mary hugged her, "You decided to come back to us."

"Of course we did, dear." Mother smiled. "We missed you very much."

"What did I tell you?" Grandpa David said.

"Did you think we would decide not to come back?" Their father looked astonished.

"Of course not," Billy said. "We knew you wanted to come back." He looked at his grandfather with a little smile. Grandpa David winked at him. The children's secret was safe with him. ✻

Grandpa David Williams' Think Box

❑ What was Frederick Douglass's real name and why did he change it?

❑ How did Frederick escape and why was he almost caught again?

❑ Who were the people whom Frederick Douglass worked with to end slavery and how did it end?

○ What was life like as a slave? What does the Bible say about slavery?

Harriet Beecher Stowe

Unlocking Uncle Tom's Cabin

Mary slowly walked down the stairs.
She carried her favorite doll, Matilda.
When she reached the bottom of the stairs, she
sat down on the last step. A few minutes later,
her mother found her there hugging Matilda
tightly. "What's the matter, Precious? I thought

you were playing with your brother."

"I don't want to play with him. He wanted to play a mean game," Mary said.

"What kind of mean game, dear?" her mother asked as she sat down next to Mary. "What was he playing?"

"He wanted me to be his slave. That was his game. He ordered me around. I did chores. I cooked and cleaned and milked cows and stuff like that."

"That doesn't sound like a nice game." Mom was frowning.

"And after that, he was mean to me," Mary continued. "When I said he should be nice, he said that wasn't part of the game."

"I think someone needs a talking to." Mom stood and called up the stairs. "William, please come down here, now!"

"Okay, Mom," Billy said slowly. Mary could tell that he knew he was in trouble. Mother only called him William when he was in trouble.

Billy came down the stairs slowly. He looked a little worried.

"I've been hearing about the game you were playing," his mother said.

Billy didn't say anything.

"You weren't treating your sister very nicely, were you?" his mother went on.

"That was just part of the game," Billy said.

"If playing a certain game means being mean to people, you should play a different game," his mother said. "Isn't that right?"

"Yes, Mom," Billy answered.

"Besides, slavery is not a good game to play. Slavery is a very bad thing. You know that, don't you, William?" his mother asked.

"I guess so," Billy nodded.

"Mommy, what was real slavery like?" Mary wanted to know.

"Some people used to own other people. It was just like owning a dog, a horse, or a machine. People had slaves to do the jobs they didn't want to do themselves," their mother explained.

"Were people mean to their slaves?" Mary asked.

"Many times they were," said her mother. "One of the meanest things a person can do is to treat someone else like he isn't a real person."

Mary shook her head. "I can't believe people really acted like that."

"It is hard to understand," said Mom, "but it happened often. There used to be many slaves in America."

"Didn't anyone know it wasn't a nice way to act?" asked Mary.

"Some people did. It's partly because of those people that we don't have slavery any more in this country. I can tell you the story of a woman who fought against slavery. Would you like to hear it?"

"Yes, please. " Mary changed the way she was holding Matilda so the doll could hear the story too.

This is the story of Harriet Beecher Stowe. Harriet was born in Connecticut in 1812. She was the sixth child to be born to the Beecher family. Her father was a poor preacher, and life was sometimes hard.

Harriet started school when she was five. She was good in school. When she was fifteen, she started working as a teacher in the school run by her older sister.

Her father moved to Cincinnati not long after that. Harriet and her sister Catherine went to Ohio with their father. There they opened a new school.

In 1833, she took a trip. Harriet was then twenty-one. She and another teacher from her school went to Kentucky. In Kentucky, she saw slavery for the first time. She was shocked. There hadn't been any slavery in Connecticut or Ohio when she was growing up.

"Did you see the way they make their slaves live?" Harriet asked her friend on the way back to Cincinnati.

"Yes, I did," her friend replied. "It is horrible."

"The slaves are all crowded together in those little shacks," Harriet went on. "I never heard anyone speak a kind word to any of them during our whole visit."

"I know."

"They work them and work them until the slaves just can't work any more." Harriet was so upset that she wasn't listening to her friend. "The slaves are treated more like animals than people. Something must be done."

Harriet didn't know what to do about slavery. There were so many slaves in so many states. What could one person do against such a big problem?

Back in Ohio, Harriet started working at being an author. She published her first story in 1834. Two years later, she married Calvin Stowe. Calvin was a teacher at the college where her father worked. For many years, the Stowe family remained poor. Calvin did not earn much money as a teacher. Harriet sold stories to newspapers and magazines and that helped.

In 1850, Calvin got a job with a better salary at Bowdoin College in Maine. At last, Harriet could work on a story that she had wanted to tell for a long time. The year after the Stowes moved to Maine, Harriet published the first part of her great work.

Her new book was called *Uncle Tom's Cabin*. It was about the terrible way slaves were treated. She based the book on the plantation she had visited in Kentucky.

The book was very popular. Many people who had never lived in areas where there was slavery read the book. They had no idea how bad it was. Before Harriet's book, only a few people spoke out publicly against slavery. Many more people joined the anti-slavery movement after reading her story. *Uncle Tom's Cabin* helped to end slavery in this country. When people knew the truth about how things were, they couldn't let it go on. They couldn't stand the thought of people being treated like the ones in Harriet's book.

Harriet had finally found something to do about the problem of slavery. She found a way to make a change. However, Harriet never took credit for the book. She felt God had used her to write it. She said, "I could not control the story; the Lord Himself wrote it. I was but an instrument in His hands and to Him should be given all the praise."

Harriet died in 1896. She lived long enough to see the end of slavery in this country. She also knew that her book had been an important part of the fight to free the slaves.

"Maybe I should read that book to you kids," their mother said. "I think that would be a better way to spend your time than playing slavery. Would you like that?"

"That would be fine," Mary answered.

"We'll start tonight," said Mom. "Now, you children go and play until dinner is ready. Do you think you can play a better game this time?"

Billy nodded. "Yes, Mom. I don't want to play slavery any more." ❦

Katherine Anderson's Think Box

❏ What did Harriet think about slavery?

❏ What did she do about it?

❏ How did her book *Uncle Tom's Cabin* help make slaves free?

O Words can be powerful! Are you learning how to use words well? If you were to write a book, what would you write about?

Susan B. Anthony

Swimming Against the Current

When their parents' car pulled into the driveway, Billy and Mary ran up to meet them. "Why are you two so wet?" their mother asked as she got out of the car.

"Did it rain here while we were at the store?" asked their father. He began to take the groceries out of the trunk.

Mary giggled. "It didn't rain."

"We washed Grandpa's car," Billy explained.

"That was a nice thing to do," Mom smiled.

"It looks more like you washed each other," said their father.

"Well, maybe a little," said Mary. "You always say that Billy doesn't do a very good job on his own." She started laughing.

Billy ignored his sister's joke. "Do you want to see what Grandpa gave us for doing such a good job?"

"You need to go change out of those wet clothes first," Mom said.

"Aw, Mom," Billy complained.

"Go ahead," their father said. "Do what your mother said."

"And don't just throw those wet clothes on the floor," Mom added. "Hang them up in the bathroom. Then you can show us what you got from your grandfather."

A little while later the two children came back downstairs in dry clothes. "Now, what treasures did you get from Grandpa?" their mother asked.

Billy reached into his pocket and pulled out a large coin. "He gave us each one of these. Grandpa said that they were dollars, but I've never seen ones like these before."

His father took the coin out of Billy's hand and looked at it. "This is a Susan B. Anthony dollar."

"Is it a real dollar?" Billy asked.

"Yes it is," his father answered. "It's genuine coin of the realm, accepted everywhere."

"Is that Susan B. Anthony's face on the coin?" Mary wanted to know.

Mom nodded. "That's right, dear."

"Was she president or something?" Mary asked.

"No, dear," her mother said. "We haven't had a woman president yet."

"Who was she, then?" Mary asked. "I thought everybody on money was a president."

"Most of our money has pictures of our presidents, but Susan B. Anthony wasn't even a politician. She worked so that maybe some day we can have a woman for our president."

"How did she do that? What did she do?" Now Billy was getting interested.

"Why don't you two have a seat and I'll tell you her story," said their mother.

Susan B. Anthony was born in 1820 to a wealthy family in Massachusetts. Her father owned a cotton mill that made cloth. Cotton cloth was becoming very popular, and Susan's father did very well. She was the second oldest of six children.

Susan's family were Quakers. In Quaker meetings, men and women were equal.

Anyone could stand up and speak as long as he had something to say. Women could even take part in voting on church questions. This was long before they were allowed to vote for the political leaders of the country. The idea that men and women are equal was not held by very many people at that time. A lot of people still aren't sure about that idea. Quaker feelings about the equality of men and women were based on a simple idea. Whether you are a man or woman, you're still a person; and all people should be treated the same.

The Quakers had the same idea about African Americans. It didn't matter whether you were black or white, people are people. All people should have the same rights. Susan grew up before the Civil War. At that time, many people still owned slaves. The Quakers were some of the first people to speak out against slavery. People who worked to end slavery were called abolitionists because they wanted to abolish, or end, it. It was in the Abolitionist Movement that Susan B. Anthony first became a fighter.

Both of her parents were free-thinkers. That meant that they made up their own minds about things and had different ideas than many other people. Susan shared her parents' ideas. When she was growing up, Susan didn't know that she was going to become one of this country's most famous fighters for freedom and justice. But she wasn't just an ordinary little girl either. Even when she was quite young, everyone could see how smart she was. When Susan was four years old, her grandmother taught her to read.

When she was still a young woman, she outgrew the school in her hometown. She had already learned all that her teacher could teach her. Luckily, Susan's father was determined to let her learn all she could. He set up a school in the Anthony home. There he taught his children, as well as many of the women who worked in his cotton mill. This was another way that Susan B. Anthony was different from most women of her time. Very few people thought it was important for women to go to school. Women only needed to know how to sew and keep house. That's what most people thought, anyway.

By the time Susan was 29 years old, she had finished going to school and had become a teacher in another town. She was a very good teacher. The problem was that soon she was bored with it. It was too easy for her. She wanted to do something new and difficult, but she had no idea what that could be. She went back to her parents' home in 1849 and hoped she would find something interesting to do with the rest of her life. When she got there, she found what she was looking for.

Right away she started working to change America in three very important ways. She had heard a lot about the first two problems while she was growing up. Her parents had always been concerned about slavery. The Anthony home became a meeting place for people who were working to end slavery. She talked with many famous abolitionists including Frederick Douglass, who had once been a slave himself. Another cause that her parents had always felt strongly about was temperance. Temperance means not drinking alcohol. The Anthony family and many others thought that these drinks should be illegal. They were concerned because many men who drank too much became violent with their wives and children. Susan joined groups which protested, held rallies, and made speeches trying to convince politicians to end slavery and make alcoholic beverages illegal.

Most people remember Susan B. Anthony for the third way she tried to make the United States a better place to live. However, this is the one she was least sure about. In 1848, a year before Susan went back home, some women held a meeting and demanded the right to vote. Susan thought this was going too far. It surprised her that her father agreed with this idea. She decided to meet the woman in charge of the group that had made this demand. That woman's name was

Elizabeth Cady Stanton. Elizabeth and Susan became very good friends right away. Not long after that, Susan started working for women's suffrage. Suffrage is the right to vote.

"How did Susan and Elizabeth fight to change things?" asked Mary.

"Did they start a war or something?" Billy asked.

"No," answered Mom. "Of course, they didn't start a war. They fought with words."

Elizabeth wrote speeches, and Susan traveled all over the place reading them. They tried to convince people to change their minds. At one time, the two women published a newspaper called "The Revolution." There weren't enough people who wanted to read it, so it only lasted two years. However, they didn't quit. They kept trying, and at last they did change things.

Slavery was the first problem which Susan had fought to solve. It was finally solved because of a war, but not one that Susan B. Anthony or Elizabeth Stanton had started. The Civil War brought about the Emancipation Proclamation which freed the slaves in the rebellious southern states. A little later, the Thirteenth Amendment to the Constitution ended all slavery in the United States.

The battle for which Susan B. Anthony is most famous, to give women the right to vote, was not completed while she was alive. She died in 1906 when she was 86 years old. Throughout her long life, she never slowed down. She was always on the road, traveling from one place to another to give her speeches. In the end, it was her younger friends who finished the work she had begun. In 1919, the Nineteenth Amendment to the Constitution was passed which gave women the right to vote. And in 1920, one hundred years after her birth, American women were finally allowed to take part in a national election.

"So, Susan B. Anthony is really a hero only for women," Billy was a little disappointed.

"No, of course not," his father said. "No more than the people who worked to end slavery are heroes for only African Americans. They all made America a better place to live."

Mary asked, "Can I vote then?"

"No, dear," answered her mother. "You have to be eighteen years old to vote."

"That's not fair," Mary said.

"Maybe you should try to be like Susan," her father suggested. "You can start making speeches to convince people to change their minds. Maybe you can make America a better place to live in, too." ❦

❏ Who taught Susan to read when she was very young?

❏ What did most people think girls should learn to do?

❏ What does "women's suffrage" mean?

○ Think of many reasons it is important to get a good education. What are some of the things you can do now to become well-educated?

Harriet Tubman

Underground Railroad Conductor

Mom heard Billy laughing. She looked out the window and saw him tugging his Aunt Anne towards the house.

Aunt Anne, Billy, and his sister Mary had gone to the park that afternoon. Katherine Anderson hadn't expected to see her children home before dinner time. It was usually very hard to get them to leave the park. But it was only about 3:00 now. They were home early. Katherine wondered if there was something wrong. She opened the front door as they came up the front steps.

Billy was holding on to one of his aunt's hands. He said, "Do you want to see my trucks now? They're up in my room."

"You go on, Billy. I'll be up in a minute," Aunt Anne said. "Let me say hello to your mother first."

"Okay, but please hurry." Billy ran up the stairs to his room.

Mother looked at Mary. "What's the matter, dear?" she asked. "Didn't you have fun at the park?"

"No." Mary went into the living room and sat on the couch.

"What happened, Anne?" Mother wanted to know.

"We met some children who weren't very nice," replied Aunt Anne. "I think Mary would like to talk to you about it. I'll go upstairs and see Billy's trucks."

Mom went into the living room and sat on the couch beside Mary. "What happened at the park today, my precious?"

"Some big kids started calling us names."

"Kids were calling you and Billy names?" her mother asked.

"No," said Mary, "not me and Billy, me and my new friend Claire."

Mother looked puzzled. "Claire? Did you just meet her today at the park?"

"Yes. We were playing on the swings when the older kids started yelling at us. They called her names and said I shouldn't play with her. They kept throwing little rocks at us when no one was watching." Tears began to roll down Mary's cheeks. "We didn't do anything to them," she said.

"Why were they being so mean?"

"Because Claire is black. They called her bad names. Why do people have to be so mean, Mommy? Claire is my friend. Aunt Anne decided we had to leave. We walked Claire to her house on the way."

"That was nice of you to walk her home," Mom said. "I'm sorry that you and Claire met people like that. Some people just don't understand what's important. It doesn't matter what people look like. Being nice to people and having friends is important."

"I know," Mary said. "Claire is nice and she is friendly. Why are people so mean?"

"It takes a long time for some people to learn what's important," Mom said. "Come over here close, and I'll tell you a story. It's about a woman who tried to teach people that the color of a person's skin doesn't show whether she is good or bad. Some people learned from her. Other people haven't learned yet."

Mary scooted over close to her mother. Mary's mother put her arm around Mary. She dried Mary's tears and brushed the hair from Mary's eyes.

This is the story of Harriet Tubman. Harriet was a slave. There used to be a law in this country that one person could own another person just like they could own a table or a dog. We no longer have that law. Now one person cannot own another person. Slavery ended because of the Civil War. During the Civil War, President Abraham Lincoln made a new law which put an end to slavery.

However, Harriet Tubman was born before slavery ended. She was born in Maryland in the year 1820. Slaves weren't important enough for people to remember their birthdays, so no one knows exactly what day she was born.

While Harriet was growing up, she didn't think much about being a slave. That was just the way things were. White people could own black people. That was the law. She, like most people, didn't think about how she lived. You probably never think about how lucky you are, my dear, to live in a nice house on a nice street.

Everything changed for Harriet when she was fifteen. There was a day she found out what it really meant to be a slave. On that day, she decided she wanted to be free. Harriet was working inside. She was glad to be out of the hot sun. She was measuring flour from a big bag into smaller bags. There was another slave from her farm in the shed where Harriet was working. His name was Gabe. He was hiding in the cool shade because he didn't want to work in the hot fields. Gabe was funny, and Harriet liked him. That day he was making her laugh by telling jokes about the overseer. The overseer was the man who made sure the slaves worked as hard as they could. "Y'all get back to work now, you hear?" Gabe said. He could sound just like the overseer.

Too late Harriet saw the overseer coming. She had no chance to warn Gabe. The overseer came into the shed and started whipping Gabe. Then, the overseer called out to Harriet, "Bring me that rope. I'm going to tie this slave to the whipping post and punish him proper."

Harriet couldn't move. She didn't want Gabe to be whipped. Gabe saw his chance to get away. He ran out of the shed. The overseer picked up his gun and started after Gabe. Harriet knew he would shoot Gabe. Quickly, she moved in front of the overseer. They both fell down, and Gabe was able to get away. From that day on, Harriet worked against the people who owned her. She worked very carefully. She knew if she was found out, she would be killed.

A few years later she learned a terrible secret. A lawyer told her that her grandparents had been set free. The law about slaves said that the children of free people were not slaves. Since her grandparents had been free, that meant her mother had been free. Since her mother had been free, Harriet was free as well. But no one had ever told her mother that she was free. Harriet's mother had been treated like a slave all of her life, and so had Harriet. She learned how wicked some people can be. The same week Harriet learned this secret, she ran away. In the North, she could be free.

Not long after Harriet Tubman started to live as a free person, she decided to help others do the same thing. Between 1850 and 1860, she helped thousands of slaves escape from the South. She would sneak back into Maryland or Virginia. She traveled at night so that she wouldn't be seen and caught. Harriet would visit plantations and gather together all of the slaves that were willing to try to be free. Then they would sneak back into the northern states. Harriet got the nickname "Moses" because, like Moses, she led her people to freedom.

Sometimes the trips to the North and freedom would take several days. Harriet had help on these trips. The Southerners who did not like slavery helped Harriet and other groups of escaping slaves. They offered their houses as hiding places, called safehouses. The trail of safehouses was called the Underground Railroad.

Harriet didn't stop working on the Underground Railroad until 1861 when the Civil War started. Soon the whole country was fighting about whether the slaves should be set free. In 1863, President Lincoln made a new law called the Emancipation Proclamation. It said that all of the slaves in the rebelling states were now free men and women.

The northern states won the Civil war. Slavery was gone from the United States, but that wasn't the end of all of the problems for people who had been slaves. Harriet Tubman and other former slaves couldn't understand why winning their freedom wasn't enough. People still looked down on former slaves. It was hard for them to get jobs. When they did get jobs, they were usually paid less.

"Negroes, or African Americans, still have many problems in this country. You saw some of them today, Mary. Many people still look down on African Americans and think of them as somehow less good than white people. The best thing you can do is to ignore what they say. You can decide for yourself who you want to be your friends. It doesn't matter what those people think. Are you going to play with Claire again?" Mary's mother asked.

Mary nodded. "Yes, I am. I like her. Maybe she won't want to play in the park, though."

"Maybe not," Mom agreed, "but maybe she'd like to come over for dinner."

Mary grinned. "Good idea! I'll ask her. Thanks, Mom." ❦

Aunt Anne's Think Box

❑ What did it mean to be a slave? What rights did a slave have?

❑ How did Harriet first save a slave from being whipped?

❑ What nickname did people give Harriet and why?

○ What would it be like to be a slave?

○ The color of a person's skin has nothing to do with whether he is good or bad. How would you feel if someone were unkind to you just because he did not like the way you looked?

John Brown

To Free the Slaves

Billy heard the front door close downstairs. His father was home.
He was sitting alone in his room where his mother had sent him. "You can just think about what you've done. You'll need to talk about it with your father when he gets home."

Billy had thought about it all afternoon, but he still could not figure out why he was being punished. He had just been helping his little sister, Mary.

Now he heard footsteps on the stairs and a knock at his door. "Are you ready to have that talk?" his father asked.

"Yes, I guess so," Billy answered.

His father came in and sat on the bed. "Why don't you tell me what happened?"

"We were all playing outside. There was Mary and me, Tommy and Scott from next door, and Brian from down the street. We were playing tag. Brian can't run very fast, so he kept getting tagged. He got mad when even Mary could tag him. He hit her. I shouted at him, and he ran away. I caught up with him in his yard and hit him back. His mother saw me and brought me back here and told Mom what I had done. I tried to explain, but Mom wouldn't listen. I was just getting him back for hitting Mary. Can't I even help my own sister?" Billy became more and more upset as he told his story. He was almost crying by the time he finished.

His father put his arm around Billy. "Yes, you are supposed to help your sister, but not by doing something bad. This may be hard to understand. Some things are wrong even when they are done for good reasons. Some wrong things are even done out of feelings of love. Let me tell you a story that may help you to understand this.

"This is a story about slavery. Now, slavery is a terrible thing. I'm going to tell you about the way one man fought against slavery. The things this man did were wrong. It didn't make them okay just because he was doing them for a good reason."

The man's name was John Brown. He was from New York State. Even though he couldn't hold a steady job, he raised twenty children.

"How would you like to have nineteen brothers and sisters?"

"I have a hard enough time with just one," Billy smiled.

His father chuckled. "I guess that's right."

John Brown was a religious man with a good heart. He knew that slavery was evil and a sin. Unfortunately, he went to terrible extremes in his fight against that evil.

John Brown lived before the American Civil War, the war that eventually ended slavery. Many people tried to end slavery before the war. These people had many different ideas on how to do this. Some of the people were peaceful. They lectured and preached that slavery was evil. Other people were violent. They attacked people who owned slaves.

Brown also did many things in his fight against slavery. In Ohio, he worked on the Underground Railroad. This was not a real railroad. It was a group of people who helped slaves escape from the southern United States and run away to Canada. In Massachusetts, John Brown met the freed slave, Frederick Douglass. In Kansas, he even killed some people. John Brown, some of his sons, and some other people wanted to stop slavery from spreading to the western states. They killed five people who owned slaves. Later, one of Brown's sons was killed in revenge for that attack.

In 1859, he had another idea. In that year, John Brown and eighteen followers attacked the town of Harpers Ferry, Virginia. Some of Brown's followers were his sons; others were freed slaves. They attacked Harpers Ferry because a United States government arsenal was located there. An arsenal is a place for storing weapons. His plan was to give the weapons to the slaves from all over the state of Virginia. He thought they would come to Harpers Ferry when they heard what he had done. Then, with this army of freed slaves, he would attack other states farther to the south.

His plan didn't work. John Brown and his raiders did gain control of the arsenal, but to do it they had to fire some shots in the night. The people of Harpers Ferry knew something had happened. They were quick to find out just exactly what it was. They came to talk to Brown in the morning.

"Who are you? What do you want?" the townspeople asked the leader of the raiders.

"My name is John Brown. I'm here to free all the slaves in this state. I am holding Colonel Lewis Washington and some others of your leading citizens as hostages," Brown answered.

Brown had not expected what would happen next. He had hoped that hundreds of escaping slaves would hurry to join him, but the slaves were unable to do this. When the local slave owners heard what John Brown had said, they locked up their slaves even tighter. Then, the slave owners gathered their own guns and attacked Brown in the arsenal. Worse than that, later that day ninety United States Marines came to Harpers Ferry from Baltimore. The marines were commanded by Colonel Robert E. Lee who would later be in charge of the Southern army during the Civil War. Right now, he was still proud to serve the United States. John Brown's eighteen men were no match for these professional soldiers. The next morning, the marines battered down the door of the arsenal and took John Brown prisoner.

Brown was put on trial for murder, treason, and rebellion. When he was asked why he had done what he did, he simply said,

"To free the slaves." In all, ten of John Brown's raiders and many townspeople were killed. He was found guilty. When the verdict was read, he said, "I believe that what I have done was not wrong, but right, because I was fighting against a great wrong." Brown was wrong about that.

One of the people who saw him executed was John Wilkes Booth. Booth would later kill President Abraham Lincoln. Lincoln managed to do what John Brown had tried to do. He freed the slaves living in the southern states. And he did it the right way, with a law.

"So you see, Billy," his father said, "there are right ways and wrong ways to do good things. Hitting Brian was the wrong thing to do. You should have told your mother or Brian's mother what had happened. Will you remember this talk and this story?"

"Yes, Dad," Billy said, "I will."

"Good. Then come downstairs. I think your mother is making something good for dinner." ❧

❑ John Brown's goal was to free the slaves. Did he go about it in the right way?

❑ Is it okay to do wrong things if it is for a good reason?

○ What do you think John Brown could have done better to help make slaves free? When you see others doing wrong things, what should you do?

Abraham Lincoln

Learning by Littles

"What are you going to do?" Billy looked at the book his sister was holding. It was soaking wet. Its pages were swelled up and bent. The book wouldn't even close any more.

"I don't know. It's ruined." Mary began to cry.

"Whose book is it?" Billy asked. "I mean, whose book was it?"

"Aunt Anne loaned it to me." Mary wiped tears from her face. "She's visiting today. What am I going to say?"

"Can you buy a new one?" asked Billy.

"No. I've spent all of my allowance already."

"Books are expensive," Billy said. "You're going to get into trouble."

"I know." Mary started crying again.

Just then their mother walked past Mary's door. She heard Mary crying and came into the room. Mary hid the ruined book behind her back.

"What's the matter, dear?" Mary's mother asked. She frowned at Billy. "Have you been teasing your sister again?"

"No," Billy said.

"Then, what's the matter?" she asked again.

Billy looked at his sister. He didn't know what to say. He didn't really want to get her into trouble.

Mrs. Anderson looked from Mary to Billy and back again. She was waiting for an answer. Finally, Mary said, "It's this." She showed her mother the book. "I was reading it while I was taking my bath, and I dropped it in the water." Mary saw her mother frowning again. "I know you told me not to do that, but it was so interesting. I didn't want to stop reading it."

"Well, I am glad that you like reading so much." Mother wasn't frowning any more. "There's no telling how much you'll be able to do if you keep being so interested in learning. What was the book about?"

"It was the story of George Washington. He was our first president," Mary said.

"That's interesting." Mary's mother sat down on the bed next to her children. "I know the story of a very great man who once ruined a book about George Washington. That book got soaking wet as well. Would you like to hear the story?" Both children wanted to hear the story, of course. They also wanted to keep their mother's mind off the book Mary had ruined.

This is a story about Abraham Lincoln. He was our sixteenth president. When he was born, no one could have known that he would be such a great man. Everything that he was able to do with his life, he did because he worked hard. He loved to learn, and he loved to read. Most of what he learned, he taught himself.

Abraham Lincoln was born in a small, one-room cabin in Kentucky. The cabin had only one window and a dirt floor. His parents didn't have much money. They were good people, and they worked hard.

Lincoln was born in February of 1809. The day he was born his cousin Dennis Hanks ran miles through the snow to see the new baby.

Abraham's skin was all red and wrinkled. Dennis thought the baby looked like a squeezed-out cherry. "Can I hold him?" Dennis asked.

"Be careful," Mrs. Lincoln said. She handed him the baby and showed him how to hold it.

While Dennis was holding little Abraham, the baby started to cry and wouldn't stop. Dennis didn't like that noise. He handed the baby back to Mrs. Lincoln. "I reckon he'll never amount to much," he said.

By the time Abraham was seven years old, he was already tall for his age. In that year his father, Tom Lincoln, moved the family to Indiana. Much of the land in Indiana was good for farming, and Tom wanted to start a new farm there. Getting from Kentucky to Indiana was much harder then than it is now. There were no roads or trains or anything like that. The Lincolns had to pack everything they wanted to take with them in a wagon. They went to their new home on horseback. Sometimes they had to go through forests. Tom Lincoln had to chop down trees to make enough room for the wagon to get through.

Finally, they reached Indiana. The first thing they had to do was clear a place in the woods for their new farm. Tom Lincoln chopped down the trees, and Abraham cut down the bushes. His father was glad to see how strong Abraham was becoming. He knew that his son would be a big help on the farm.

One of the ways Abraham tried to help his family was by hunting for food. One day, when he was only eight years old, he shot a turkey. When he saw the dead bird, Abraham became sick. He never killed another animal. No one could have known at that time that the boy who turned ill at the sight of the death of a bird would one day be Commander in Chief of a terrible war. That war was called the Civil War or the War Between the States. Many people died in that war. However, that wouldn't happen until Abraham had grown up.

Abraham Lincoln hardly went to school at all when he was growing up. That was because there was so much work to do on the farm. He went to school a little when he was six years old. He went to school a little bit more when he was seven. He didn't go back to school until he was eleven. Then he attended school a little longer when he was thirteen. The last time he went to school was when he was fifteen. All of the days he was at school wouldn't even add up to a whole year. Later on, Abraham said he went to school "by littles."

About the only thing Abraham learned in school was how to read. He loved to read. That was a good thing because almost everything he ever learned he did by reading to himself. His problem was finding books to read. His family was poor and only had a couple of books. Abraham got into the habit of borrowing books from people on neighboring farms. One time he had borrowed a book about George Washington just like you, Mary. He was up late one night reading it. Finally, he decided he had to go to bed. He put the book away in a little space between two logs in the wall of his family's house.

Well, it rained that night. Wind blew the rain through all of the gaps in the cabin walls. By morning, the book was soaking wet. Abraham didn't know what to do. He had no money to pay for it. He went to the farmer who had loaned it to him. "I've ruined your book. Please let me work for you. That way I'll be able to pay you for it."

"That'll be fine," said the farmer. "You can start by splitting enough rails for my new fence."

Abraham worked three long days. Finally, he made enough to pay the farmer for the book. The farmer let him keep the book. Even though the pages were all bent from getting wet and the cover wouldn't close, he could still read it. He read it again many times after that.

Abraham Lincoln went on reading, and he went on learning things. When he was older, he taught himself to be a lawyer. He didn't win every case, but he was a good lawyer. He wanted to help people. One time, he learned that his client had lied to him. He left the courtroom. The judge sent someone to bring him back. Lincoln said, "I can't come now. I've got to wash my hands."

Later, he decided that he could help people more if he were a politician. He didn't win every election he was in, but he was a good politician. Finally, he became president of the United States, in fact, one of our most famous presidents. When the Southern states wanted to be their own country, Lincoln didn't let them. Even though he hated death, he led the country into the Civil War to keep the United States united .

Just then a car pulled up outside the house. "That's probably Aunt Anne," Mary's mother said. "You need to decide what you're going to do about her book."

"I guess I should work for her," Mary said. "Maybe that way I can pay her back for it." She ran down the stairs to open the door for her aunt. She carried the book with her. She wasn't afraid to tell the truth about what had happened anymore.

"I reckon she won't amount to much," Billy said after his sister had left.

"That's not a very nice thing to say," his mother said.

"It worked for Abraham Lincoln," said Billy. "He became great after someone said that about him." 🌿

Mary Anderson's Think Box

❏ Did Abraham Lincoln come from a rich family? What kind of home did they have?

❏ Why was Lincoln not able to attend school much of the time?

❏ How many days did he work to pay for the book that was ruined?

○ Why was Abraham Lincoln a good president? What are some of the things he valued and respected most about other people?

Clara Barton

The Angel of the Battlefield

"**O**uch! That hurts!" Billy complained.

"Be quiet," said Mary. "I have to clean it."

"I want to go find Mom." Billy tried to edge past his sister.

"I can do this just as well as she can," Mary responded. "I've watched Mom take care of scrapes hundreds of times."

"When she does it, it doesn't hurt," said Billy.

"It does too," Mary said. "You just don't remember. You can't clean a scrape without it hurting a little."

"No, I'm sure," Billy continued. "Mom never hurts me."

"Well, whatever." Mary stepped back and looked at her brother's knee. "I'm finished with that part anyway. Now all I have to do is put a bandage on it."

Just then Grandma Brigit walked past the bathroom door. She was visiting Mary and Billy for the weekend. "What's going on here, children?" she asked.

"I fell off my bike," Billy explained. "Then Mary dragged me in here to fix my knee."

"Well, it looks like you've done a very good job," Grandma said as she looked at the now clean scrape.

Mary smiled. "Thank you."

"After hurting so much, I hope she did a good job," said Billy. Mary frowned at him.

"As I used to say to your mother when she was a little girl, you can't clean a scrape without it hurting a little," said his grandmother.

"See?" Mary's smile returned. "I told you so."

"Do you want to be a nurse when you grow up, dear?" her grandmother asked.

"I don't know." Mary shrugged. "Maybe."

"Do you like to help people?"

"I think she likes hurting people more than helping them," said Billy.

"Now you stop that, Billy. The cleaning is all finished now. Besides, you should be thanking your sister for the good job she's done. All sorts of bad things can happen if you don't clean out cuts and scrapes."

"Okay, Grandma." Billy turned to his sister. "Thanks, Mary."

"Now you go ahead and put a bandage on your brother's knee," Grandma said. "Then I will tell you a story of a very great nurse who started by caring for her brother just like you have."

Mary put the bandage on Billy's knee. He was hoping to be able to complain again, but it didn't hurt. Then the two children went to the living room to hear their grandmother's story.

This is the story of Clara Barton. Clara was born on Christmas Day in 1821 in Massachusetts. Her parents named her Clarissa, but everyone called her Clara.

When she was a little girl, Clara was very shy. "Why don't you play outside with the other children, dear?" her mother would ask.

"I'm afraid," Clara would answer.

"But what are you afraid of?" her mother would ask her.

"Everything," was always Clara's answer.

As Clara grew older, she found out that the only time she wasn't afraid was when she was helping other people.

When Clara was nine years old, her brother, David, was hurt in a fall.

"Did he fall off a bicycle?" Billy asked.

"I don't know, dear," his grandmother answered. "I don't think so."

"He probably wasn't as clumsy as you." Mary grinned but Billy frowned.

Soon after his accident, David came down with a bad fever. The doctors ordered a treatment called "bloodletting." They thought his fever was caused by "bad blood." To cure him they had to let out the bad blood. They did this with leeches. A leech is a special kind of worm which sucks blood.

Clara spent all of her time with David. She watched over him and tried to help him feel better. She was already becoming a nurse. After many weeks, David was no better. The rest of his family began to give up hope. Only Clara stayed with him. She nursed him for almost two years. Finally, his parents decided to stop using leeches. After that, he recovered quickly. The leeches had probably been keeping him weak and sick.

Doctors don't usually use leeches any more. We now know a lot more about why people get sick and how to make them better.

Clara was very glad that her brother was finally well. She did miss having a patient to nurse, though. A few years later, she had another chance to be a nurse. Smallpox, a very dangerous disease, came to her home town. Clara did all that she could to cure the sick, or at least, to make them more comfortable. This young woman, who had been afraid of everything as a child, was not afraid to go where others wouldn't in order to help the sick.

Even though Clara loved being a nurse, that was not her first real job. She became a teacher instead. She was a very good teacher. Many of her students remembered her long after they had left her class. Some wrote her letters telling her that she had changed their lives.

Clara didn't work as a nurse for many years and she missed it. Her chance came in 1861. That was the year the Civil War began. She wanted to fight to protect the Union, but women weren't allowed into the army. She would have to find some other way to help. It didn't take Clara long to decide how she could help.

She was in Washington, D.C., when a trainload of soldiers arrived. These soldiers were from her home state. The Massachusetts troops were in bad shape. They had been attacked by crowds of angry Southerners. They were ragged and many were wounded. The army couldn't help them. The army didn't have any extra clothes or medicine to give to the injured troops. Clara collected all the supplies she could buy. She also wrote letters to the parents of the soldiers asking them to send whatever they could. The troops were very grateful.

Clara learned from the soldiers how few doctors there were to care for the injured. The stories haunted her. She knew she was a good nurse. She decided to work as a nurse for the army. Proper ladies weren't supposed to go to the front lines, but she couldn't help that. She knew she had to help.

The army didn't let her nurse soldiers until 1862. The first battlefield Clara saw was Cedar Mountain in Virginia. She arrived along with a wagon full of supplies. The doctor in charge was James Dunn. He later wrote to his wife, "When I saw Miss Barton and her wagon, I thought heaven had sent us an angel." That letter was published in many newspapers across the country. From that time on, Clara Barton was known as "The Angel of the Battlefield."

Clara visited many battlefields during the war. She helped hundreds, maybe even thousands, of soldiers. Many of them remembered the brave nurse who had saved their lives. Sometimes, she barely managed to escape being captured by Southern soldiers. Whenever she was helping people, she forgot about being afraid of everything.

The war finally ended in 1865. After the war, there were thousands of soldiers who were missing. Clara wrote thousands of letters searching for information about these lost soldiers. Whenever she learned anything, she wrote the families of the soldiers. Sometimes she could write happy letters. Most of the time, though, she had sad news to pass along.

After years of hard work, Clara was exhausted. In 1869, she took a trip to Europe to rest. She had become very famous. Many people in Europe had heard about her work. In Switzerland, she learned about a group called the International Red Cross. It had been formed by several European countries who had signed the Treaty of Geneva. The Red Cross collected supplies and trained nurses during times of peace so that they would be ready to help soldiers in war. Clara thought the Red Cross was just what we needed in the United States. We had had no supplies to help soldiers during the Civil War.

Clara was surpised she had never heard of the Red Cross. She learned that the United States hadn't signed the Treaty of Geneva. People in America were afraid that if they joined a group of other countries, those countries would try to control what went on in the United States.

It took many years to convince the United States to sign the treaty. Clara finally changed the people's minds by changing what the Red Cross did. She knew that it wasn't only in war when we needed medicine and other supplies. People also needed help after natural disasters like floods and earthquakes. Clara's writings and speeches showed people how helpful the Red Cross could be. She influenced the Senate to ratify the Treaty of Geneva. In 1882, President Chester A. Arthur signed it. Clara Barton was the first president of the American Red Cross. The Red Cross still helps thousands of people every year.

"Can I join the Red Cross?" Mary asked when her grandmother had finished the story.

"I think you're a little young yet," her grandmother answered, "but we can get some books about other doctors and nurses for you from the library. Then you'll be ready when you get a little older."

"Good!" Billy grinned. "That will give her time to practice not hurting people so much."

"Billy!" Mary warned him. "You should be glad I don't have to nurse you for two whole years." Billy groaned and rolled his eyes at that thought. ❧

❏ What did Clara do that helped her not to feel afraid?

❏ Tell about several things that Clara did to help the soldiers.

❏ After the war, what did Clara do for the families of the soldiers?

◯ The Red Cross does many things to help people. Find out about things they have done to help people in recent months. Think about how important it is for people to help others. What would happen if nobody was willing to help others?

Robert E. Lee
The Gentleman's General

All the way home in the car, Billy didn't
say a word. He just stared out the
window. Even his sister, Mary, who would
normally have teased him, didn't bother him.

His team had lost the last soccer match of
the year. Now they wouldn't be in the finals. As

soon as they arrived home, Billy went upstairs to his room and closed the door.

When Uncle Bob and Aunt Anne came over later that day for dinner, Billy was still in his room. Uncle Bob went up to see him.

Bob knocked on the door. "William, can I come in?"

"Okay," said Billy in a small voice.

Uncle Bob opened the door and sat down on the bed next to Billy. "I heard you had a disappointing day today."

"Yes." Billy still wasn't much in the mood to talk.

"Did your team let you down?"

"No, they all played fine. It was me, mostly. I'm the captain, you know. I'm supposed to be the best one. But I just couldn't do anything right. I let everybody down."

Billy had thought that talking about it would make him feel worse. That was why he had stayed in his room. But as he talked, he felt better. There was something about having Uncle Bob around that helped.

"You may not believe it," his uncle said when Billy finished, "but you sound like a hero to me."

Billy looked up suddenly and stared at Uncle Bob. "How can I be a hero? You can't be a hero if you lose."

"Being a hero isn't about winning or losing, William," Uncle Bob explained. "It's about how a person acts. Here you are, feeling rotten about losing the game, but you're not trying to blame other people. You were the leader of that team. And like the best leaders, you are taking the responsibility on yourself. You remind me of another hero who also suffered defeat. That was Robert E. Lee. He led the Southern army during the American Civil War."

"His name is like yours, Uncle Bob. Bob is short for Robert. Were you named after Robert E. Lee?" Billy asked.

"I don't know. But if I were, I certainly wouldn't mind. This story will show you why."

By the end of the Civil War, the South was running out of everything it needed to keep fighting. Most of the factories were in the North, so the Northern army had all the guns and bullets it needed. But the South couldn't make enough of these things for itself. The North also had a lot of strong ships. They used them to guard the ports so the South was not able to bring in by ship the things it couldn't make for itself. Finally, the Southern army ran out of the thing it needed most of all. That was food.

In April of 1865, the last big army of the South had to leave Richmond, Virginia. They had been guarding that city from the Northern army. The Southerners headed west hoping to find food and a place to rest so they could fight again. The Northern army stayed right behind them. The Southerners had no chance to stop marching and rest. Finally, at a town called Appomattox Court House, the Southern army stopped. Their general, Robert E. Lee, wanted to save the lives of as many of his men as possible. At that town he sent a message to the general of the Northern army, Ulysses S. Grant. Lee said he was ready to surrender. His army had no more food and couldn't go on.

"Appomattox Court House is a strange name for a town," Billy said.

Uncle Bob nodded. "It was a small town. There was the county court house, a few stores, and a small number of farm houses. That's all there was."

The Southern army was camped just north of town. Early in the afternoon of April 9, Colonel Babcock, on orders from General Grant, rode into the Southerners' camp. He found General Lee resting under an apple tree.

"Are you ready to meet with General Grant, sir?" Babcock asked.

Lee was only fifty-seven, but his gray hair and beard made him look older. "Yes, son, take me to him." He mounted his horse, Traveler. Together Babcock, Lee, and Lee's aide, Colonel Marshall, rode into the small town.

The three officers looked for a place to have the meeting between Lee and Grant. They met a farmer named Wilmer McLean on the street. "Excuse me, sir," Colonel Babcock said to him. "Do you know of a place where we can hold a meeting?"

"There is a vacant house just down the street, but it has no furniture," McLean answered.

"That's not quite what we had in mind," Colonel Marshall said. "Is there no other place?"

Reluctantly Wilmer McLean said, "Well, you can use my house. It's this brick one here."

The officers thanked him. The two Southerners went into the parlor to wait. Colonel Babcock went to fetch General Grant.

Wilmer McLean had an interesting story himself. Four years earlier, he had owned a farm near the town of Manassas, Virginia. His house was next to a creek called the Bull Run. That was the site of the first battle of the Civil War. McLean's house was destroyed during that battle. He had moved, hoping to avoid having anything more to do with the war. Now his property would be used by the armies again. This time, it was to end the war.

Grant soon arrived at McLean's house with several of his officers.

"What are your terms, sir?" General Lee asked.

General Grant had a great respect for General Lee. He did not want to make him feel any worse than he already did. "Merely that all of your men surrender. They must turn in all of their weapons and equipment," Grant said. Then he noticed that Lee was wearing a very fancy sword. He thought it was probably an heirloom of the Lee family.

"These terms do not include personal weapons," Grant added. He was letting Lee keep his family's sword.

"Many of my men have used their own horses and mules," said General Lee.

"These terms will not include the animals owned by your men When these terms have been met, your men are free to return to their homes and farms."

General Lee thanked General Grant. "Those are generous terms. My men would not be able to take up farming again without their animals. We are holding about a thousand of your men as prisoners. I will arrange to return them at once because we have no food and we cannot feed them."

When Grant heard that, he quickly made arrangements for food to be taken to the Southerners' camp. After the agreement had been signed by both sides, the officers each went back to their own camp.

General Lee spent the rest of that day arranging for the surrender. Then he rode once more through the camp. His men saw that the reins on his horse were loose. The horse guided itself towards Lee's tent. The men raised a cheer for their leader. When they saw tears rolling down his cheeks and into his beard, they all started to cry.

"We still love you as much as ever," one old soldier shouted. The men cheered again.

When he got to his tent, Lee turned and said, "I've done the best I could for you, but I've let you down. Go home now and be good citizens. I shall always be proud of you."

"Lee was a hero, Billy," Uncle Bob said. "Even though he lost, he thought first of his men. He blamed himself. Everyone still respected him. Now come on downstairs and have dinner with a bunch of people who still respect you."

Billy smiled at his uncle. Together, they went downstairs. ❧

Uncle Bob Anderson's Think Box

❑ Near the end of the war General Lee was concerned about his men. Why?

❑ Where did the two generals meet to discuss the surrender of the Southern army?

❑ In what ways did General Grant show respect to General Lee?

O Why did Billy think General Lee was a hero? What character traits does it take to become a true hero?

Mark Twain

Life on the Mississippi

"**O**kay, kids, everybody wake up now," Dad called out over his shoulder to the back seat of the car. Billy and his sister, Mary, were fast asleep. They didn't wake up. Mom had to turn around in her seat and shake them.

"What is it?" Billy asked. "Are we there yet?"

"We are not there yet," his father answered. "We won't be there for awhile. There's something I want you to see. We're about to cross Old Man River."

"Old Man who?" Mary asked sleepily.

"Old Man River," Dad repeated. "That's a nickname for the Mississippi River."

"Why do they call it that?" Mary asked.

"Because it's so big," her mother explained, "that it moves slowly just like an old man."

"Like Grandpa George in the morning," Billy laughed.

"Be nice," his mother reminded him.

"Sorry."

"Here it is," Dad said as they started across the bridge.

Mary was wide awake now. "It's so big! It's like an ocean."

"Well, it's not quite as big as the ocean," Mom said. "It is a very big river."

"Do we have time to stop and look at it for awhile?" Billy asked.

"Of course," his father nodded. "That's one of the good things about starting a trip so early in the morning."

"And I thought it was just so the kids would sleep in the car," Mom said.

"That, too," Dad smiled.

When they reached the other side of the bridge, they saw a sign for a rest area. Dad pulled the car into the parking lot, and Billy and Mary jumped out. They raced each other down to the bank of the river. They were just in time to see a paddle-wheeler come around a bend in the river and head toward them.

Mary pointed. "Look at that funny boat."

"I wish we could ride on it," said Billy.

Their parents reached the river just in time to hear Billy say that. "We have another Mark Twain here," his father said.

"Who is Mark Twain?" Billy wanted to know.

"Do you remember the story of Tom Sawyer?" Dad asked. "I read that story to you two not long ago."

"I remember that story," Mary said excitedly. "Tom tricked all of his friends into painting the fence his aunt wanted him to paint."

"That was a great story," added Billy. "He had a camp on an island in the middle of the river. And he made his own raft to get out to it."

"That's right," Dad said. "The person who wrote that story was Mark Twain. When he was a boy, his life was a lot like Tom Sawyer's. He grew up not far from here. He dreamed of riding on the riverboats just like you two. Would you like to hear his story?"

"We always like to hear stories," Mary said. Everyone sat down on the grass next to the wide river and listened to Dad's story.

Mark Twain was born in 1835, but he wasn't born with the name Mark Twain. His real name was Samuel Clemens. Only later, when he started writing, did he begin calling himself Mark Twain. He didn't use his real name because he worried people wouldn't like what he wrote. He didn't have anything to worry about. People have always loved his books.

When Sam was a boy, he was much like Tom Sawyer, like I just said. He went from one adventure to another. He and his friends had a favorite place to play. That was the Mississippi River. Sometimes they swam in it. At other times, they built rafts or floated on logs and crossed the wide river many times. They didn't always make it all the way across. Sam had to be rescued from the river at least nine times before he was fifteen years old. It's a miracle that he lived long enough to write his stories!

All of the boys dreamed about working on the riverboats. For Sam, the dream would actually come true for awhile. However, he tried many other jobs first. When he was still young, he worked for a newspaper called the Hannibal Courier. Most of the time he set type so that the papers could be printed. He started writing during this time.

After three years on the newspaper, he ran away to New York City to see the Exposition. The Exposition was like a big fair with exhibits about new scientific discoveries and about many foreign countries. Sam loved it and learned all he could. He also heard

about a recent expedition to map the Amazon
River in South America. He decided he
would go down there and finish the job. It
would be his greatest adventure so far.

When he reached New Orleans, he found
he didn't have nearly enough money to go to
South America. Sam was even more
discouraged when he was told it would be
eight years before another ship would sail for
the Amazon. Now, he had to find something
else to do. He was still thinking about the
Amazon. There had to be a way for him to
make a living until another boat would go to
South America. Sam decided his boyhood
dream of working on the riverboats was the
answer.

New Orleans is at the mouth of the
Mississippi River. All of the riverboats ended
up there. It took some doing, but after a while
he found a riverboat pilot who agreed to
teach him what he needed to know. It was
while working on riverboats that he got the
name that made him famous. "Mark twain" is
something that boatmen said when they
measured the depth of the river. The water
needed to be deep enough that the boats
wouldn't run aground.

Sam worked on the riverboats for five
years, then the Civil War started. It was no
longer safe for people to travel on the river.
Sam had to find something else to do. He
went to the Nevada Territory with his brother.

That was before Nevada became a state. Many people were getting rich working in the silver mines there. Sam tried his luck with silver mining, but his luck was all bad. He was soon so poor that he had to get a job in a quartz mill. Quartz is a very hard rock, and Sam's job was to break it up into small pieces. It was difficult work. After working only a week in the mill, he went to the boss to ask for a raise. This is how Sam told the story of what happened.

"He said he was paying me ten dollars a week and thought it a good round sum. How much did I want?

"I said about four hundred thousand dollars a month, and board, was about all I could reasonably ask, considering the hard times. I was ordered off the premises! And yet, when I look back to those days and call to mind the exceeding hardness of the labor I performed in that mill, I only regret that I did not ask him for seven hundred thousand."

"Sam was making a joke," Dad explained. "He thought the work was too hard for anyone to do. That's why he asked for such an incredible amount of money."

So now Sam had to find something new to do. While he was in Nevada he wrote some stories that people liked. He became a full-time writer. His first book was called

Roughing It. It was about his adventures in Nevada. It was in this book he told the story about working in the quartz mill. The book was quite funny. Finally, he had found the right job. He wrote many more books over the next few years.

Samuel Clemens, using the name Mark Twain, became famous all over the world. As a young man, he had been excited to learn about many foreign countries at the New York Exposition. Now, the people of many of these countries were excited to learn about him. Two of his fans in America wrote him a letter, but they didn't know where to send it. Sam moved around so much that no one knew where he would be. They finally addressed the letter to "Mark Twain, God Knows Where." Later, they received a telegram that simply said, "He did."

In the year Samuel Clemens was born, Halley's Comet was seen in the sky. This comet comes around about every 75 years. Sam was always sure that he would live long enough to see it again. "The comet brought me here, and it will take me away again when I'm done." He was right. Mark Twain died in 1910, the year the comet came back.

"So do we get to ride on the riverboat, Daddy?" Mary asked.

"I'm afraid not, dear," her mother answered. "That's a childhood dream that will have to go unfulfilled for now."

"Please?" Billy begged.

"Your mother is right," Dad answered. "We got up early enough to hear a story. We didn't get up early enough to float down Old Man River."

"Grandma Brigit and Grandpa David are waiting for us," Mom said. "Let's get going."

The two children walked slowly back to the car. For awhile they sat quietly in the back seat. Their parents knew something was wrong. Then Mom got an idea. She folded a couple of paper hats out of the newspaper she had been reading. She gave the hats to the children and suggested they pretend they were on the riverboat they had seen. Billy and Mary liked that idea. They took turns giving orders and steering their boats. Every time the car went over a bridge, they yelled out "mark twain" and guessed how deep the water was. ❧

❑ What was Mark Twain's real name and why didn't he use it?

❑ Mark Twain tried many new jobs before he became a writer. Name some of them.

❑ What kind of stories did Samuel Clemens write? Why did he become famous?

❍ Samuel Clemens loved adventure. Are you an adventurous person, too? What are some of the problems that can result from being adventurous?

James Butler Hickok
Wild Bill

Billy and his new friend, Lisa, were
building sand castles. Both of their
families were visiting the beach that weekend.

The children had started building their sand
castles just after lunch. Lisa had been having
trouble with hers until Billy showed her how to

mix the sand with water. The wet sand held together well. The two castles were getting very tall.

Billy and Lisa were taking turns going down to the ocean to fill their buckets with water.

"We need more water," said Lisa. "Go and get some more."

"I went last time. It's your turn," answered Billy.

"Are you sure you got it last time?" Lisa didn't wait for an answer. She picked up the two buckets and ran down to the ocean. The water was getting farther and farther away.

While Lisa was getting the water a little boy that Billy didn't know came running along the beach. When he saw Lisa's castle without anyone near it, he ran right into it. Her sand castle was now just a pile of sand with footprints in it.

Billy was very surprised by what the other boy had done. "Hey, stop that! Get away from here," he yelled. He chased him away.

Lisa came back from the ocean crying. She had seen what the boy had done. She had even forgotten their buckets of water.

"Don't worry, Lisa. I'll help you build it again."

She stopped crying when she heard this. "Thank you, Billy," she said. He ran down to the water to get their buckets.

Lisa and Billy hadn't been working on her

castle very long when the little boy came back with a couple of bigger boys.

"Are you the kid that yelled at my little brother?" the biggest boy asked.

"Yeah," said Billy. "Look what he did to Lisa's castle."

"Maybe it was in his way," the boy said. "Maybe yours is in our way." The two bigger boys went over and stomped on Billy's castle. "That'll teach you not to yell at my brother." The three boys went away laughing.

Lisa started to cry again. "Now they're both ruined. What are we going to do?"

"Come on," said Billy. "Let's go find my folks."

Billy's family were all sitting on a blanket not too far away. His father and his sister, Mary, were resting. His mother was reading a book. They hadn't seen what had happened, so Billy told them all about it.

"It was nice of you to help Lisa," Billy's mother commented.

"But I didn't really help anything," Billy complained. "Now her castle is ruined and so is mine. Maybe I shouldn't have done anything."

"It was still the right thing to do," his father said. "Sometimes it seems like there are people who just don't want others to do nice things. You did something nice, and those boys punished you for it. That is not a reason to stop doing nice things. It's too late to start rebuilding those castles today. Maybe you would feel better if you heard about another person who tried to do the right things no matter what."

"Okay," said Billy. Mary was interested now, too. The three children settled down to hear the story.

This is the story of James Butler Hickok. Later in life people called him "Wild Bill." You'll find out why in a little while.

James was born in 1837 in northern Illinois. At that time, the state was still a wild frontier. James grew up wanting to be a famous pioneer. He also wanted to do good things for people. His heroes included Davy Crockett and Sam Houston.

James knew one of the things that made his heroes famous was the fact that they were such good shots. As soon as he was old enough to carry a gun, he started practicing. By the time he was sixteen he was known as the best shot in northern Illinois.

When James was eighteen he moved to Kansas. He got a job as a constable. That's like being a city policeman. He did his job well. Not long after that James got a job driving a stagecoach. He went from Independence, Missouri, to Santa Fe, New Mexico, and back again. This was a more exciting job than being a constable because he had to go through Indian country. Being a stagecoach driver was a dangerous job.

James was always looking for more dangerous things to do. He thought that doing dangerous things would make him famous. However, he never forgot that he also wanted to help people. When he was twenty-four years old, he got a chance to do both things. That was when the American Civil War started. James chose to fight on the Northern side. He wanted to help end slavery.

He knew a lot about the territory in Kansas and Missouri, and the army knew how to use a man like James. He was given the job of scout. His mission was to find out exactly where the Southerners were. He had to creep through the back woods and along the rivers. More than once he barely managed to escape being captured.

James did so well as a scout that his commander, General Curtis, gave him an even more dangerous job. James became a spy. He pretended to be a Southerner and joined the Southern army. His mission was to find out what it was planning to do.

When he became a spy, James changed his name to Bill Barnes. This was really part of one of his brothers' names. His brother was called William Barnes Hickok.

The Southerners liked Bill Barnes. Not long after he joined, he went to work for

General Price. Price gave him some secret papers that he was supposed to deliver to another Southern general. Getting those papers was why he had become a spy. Now he had to deliver them to his own commander, General Curtis, in the North.

But how was he going to get back across the line to the Northern army? He had a plan, but it was a dangerous one. There was a man in Hickok's Southern army unit named Jake Lawson. Jake thought he was the bravest soldier in the whole South. He wasn't, though. James Hickok was. Hickok's plan depended on tricking Jake.

"Hey, Jake," Hickok said, "you think you're so brave. Why don't you go do some fighting instead of sitting around here in camp?"

"That's just what I was planning to do, Bill," Jake said. "Are you going to come with me or are you too scared?"

"I'm not scared of anything," Hickok answered.

Jake challenged him. "Let's see you prove it."

"Why don't you and I see which of us is brave and which one is scared?"

"Suits me fine," grinned Jake.

"You know the Northern army is right on the other side of the creek at the edge of our camp," Hickok said. "I bet I can ride closer to that creek than you will."

"You're on," said Jake. "I'll ride closer than anyone."

That was just what James Hickok wanted to hear. He could ride to the Northern army and none of the Southerners would try to stop him. Now he just had to keep the Northern army from stopping him.

Jake Lawson and James Hickok mounted their horses and rode as fast as they could towards the creek and the Northern army. As they neared it, the Northerners fired a few shots. Hickok started yelling at them to let him across. Jake realized he had been tricked, but he couldn't do anything about it. He had to turn around and ride back to the Southerners' camp. If he had not, he would have been shot.

James was a hero. He had delivered the secret plans of the Southern army. Because his name as a spy had been Bill Barnes and he had done some wild things, people called him "Wild Bill." That was his nickname for the rest of his life.

After the Civil War, Wild Bill Hickok became a deputy marshal in Fort Riley, Kansas. That was like being a policeman again. Now he had finally become what he always wanted to be: a famous frontiersman. He helped the people who lived on the frontier of the United States.

He was most famous for his shooting. He was the quickest and the best shot there was.

There are a lot of stories about how well he could shoot. He could shoot through the cork in a bottle without hitting the neck. He could even shoot a dime that was 150 feet away.

"You know, I don't think I could even see a dime 150 feet away," Dad said.

"No way," said Billy.

There are a couple more well-known stories about how well he could shoot. In one, Wild Bill saw a ripe apple hanging from a tree. He drew both of his guns. With the one in his left hand, he shot through the stem. With the gun in his right hand, he shot through the apple as it fell. In another story, Wild Bill was riding along with a general one day while he was still in the Northern army. He pointed out a knot on a telegraph pole. As the two men galloped past, he drew one of his guns and fired all six shots. Then, they went back to see how well Bill had done. All six shots had hit the knot.

The people of Fort Riley quickly learned how good a shot Wild Bill was. People who had thought about doing wrong changed their minds. Nobody wanted to face Wild Bill in a shoot-out.

One day he visited the town of Deadwood, South Dakota. A couple of outlaws were there who knew how dangerous Wild Bill was. They knew that they wouldn't be safe breaking the law as long as Wild Bill was around. They talked another man into shooting him in the back. Wild Bill was only thirty-nine when he died. He had been attacked because he stood up for what was right. Outlaws didn't like him because he protected people who couldn't fight for themselves.

"I liked your story, Dad," Billy said, "but it doesn't really make me want to keep doing good things. I don't want to get shot in the back like Wild Bill."

"Well, I don't think you're going to get shot for helping Lisa build a sand castle," his father replied. "Besides, that's not the point of the story. The point is that doing good and helping people is the right thing to do. You can't always worry about what might happen. Wild Bill knew that he was doing a dangerous job. But he knew that people needed his help, so he kept doing his best."

"What might happen does still worry me a little," said Billy.

"Maybe Lisa would like to stay for dinner," Billy's mother suggested.

"That would be safe," Mary teased. "You won't have to protect her from Mom's cooking."

"I'll get you for that!" Billy chased Mary back to the house where they were staying. Laughing, Lisa ran after them. ❦

Billy Anderson's Think Box

❑ James Hickok liked to do dangerous things. What were some of the jobs he did?

❑ What plan did he have for delivering secret papers to the Northern army? Did his plan work?

❑ He was most famous because he could shoot well. What are some of the stories told about him? Do you think some of the stories may have been "tall tales?"

○ Doing the right thing and protecting others is sometimes dangerous. Should you be too afraid to do the right thing? Who can help you be brave?

William Cody
Buffalo Bill

Mary came running into her grandparents' house. She and her brother,
Billy, were spending the weekend there. "Can I
have a bicycle?" she asked her grandmother.

"A bicycle, dear?"

"Yes," answered Mary. "Then I could keep

up with Billy. He always goes riding off with the other boys."

Just then Grandpa George came into the room. "A bicycle?" he asked loudly. "Now it's a bicycle she wants?"

Sometimes Grandpa would pretend to get very excited. He would wave his arms, jump around, and talk loudly. Mary thought he was funny when he acted like that. That's what he was doing now.

"You want a bicycle?" Grandpa asked again.

"Yes," Mary giggled.

"Do you know how much bicycles cost?" He was pacing back and forth through the room.

"No." Mary climbed up on the couch next to her grandmother to watch Grandpa pretend.

"Lots, that's how much," he said, waving his arms at her. "Lots and lots. This much." Grandpa stretched out his arms to show how much bicycles cost. "Do you know how much that is?"

"A lot?" Mary asked with a laugh.

"Exactly!" Grandpa almost shouted. "A lot." Grandpa seemed to calm down. He sat down in his favorite chair. "Well, there's only one way for you to get a bicycle. You'll have to go out and get a job."

Mary laughed. "I'm too young. I can't get a job."

"Too young?" He jumped up again and started to walk quickly around the living room. "You're eight years old now, aren't you?"

"Next month I'll be eight. Right now I'm still seven."

"Almost eight is close enough," Grandpa said. "No need to quibble. Almost eight is close enough. Many people have gotten jobs at your age. I know plenty of stories about famous people who got jobs when they were as old as you."

"Like who, Grandpa? Who had to work when they were as little as I am?"

"Well, there's me for one," answered Grandpa. "Did I ever tell you about how I had to chop wood and mind the animals and walk to school five miles every day in the snow?"

"Yes," said Mary, "you've told me that story. But you don't count. You're not famous."

"Don't count, do I?" Grandpa shook his head. "Okay, what about Buffalo Bill? You've heard of him, I guess. He had to work when he was eleven. That's not much more than 'almost eight.' Does he count?"

"I don't know," said Mary with a smile. She knew what her grandfather wanted her to ask. "Can you tell me his story?"

Grandpa sat down again. He crossed his legs and leaned back with a big smile. "I guess I could tell you his story."

This is the story of a boy named William Cody. The name Buffalo Bill was a prize that he won later in life. I'll tell you that part shortly. For now, it's just William.

William was born in 1846 on an Iowa farm. When William was only eight years old like you, his father, Isaac Cody, decided to move the family to California. California was supposed to be a wonderful place. Gold was found there in 1848. Cody heard that everyone got rich in California.

Even at eight, little William was not just sitting around.

"I hope you're paying close attention to this story, Mary. There are lots of good lessons to be learned," Grandpa said suddenly, pointing his finger at her.

"I am," said Mary, smiling.

Anyway, even when he was eight, William was helping to support his family. Not long after they left their Iowa farm, William shot a deer. Quite a good trick for an eight-year-old. That deer was good for many meals along the road.

When the Cody family got to Kansas, they stopped for a while. Mr. Cody wanted to find out more about California. He found some folks who had been to California but had come back. "I've heard tell that everyone can get rich in California."

They had heard the same stories. "Ain't a word of truth in it. Pack of lies, sure enough. Me and my family were there for ten years. We ain't no better off now than we used to be."

They had gone to California to get rich. It hadn't worked out. They didn't like California and had come back East. Mr. Cody decided that maybe going to California wasn't a good idea after all. The Codys settled down in Kansas.

Sadly, when William was only eleven years old, his father died. William had to help support his family again. He needed to get a job, but there weren't any jobs for young boys in Kansas. Kansas was still a rough frontier area. William had to get a man's job.

William just barely got a job herding cattle. He almost didn't get the job because he was so young. He and a group of men were to move a herd of cattle from Kansas to a ranch west of the Platte River. Everything went fine until they got close to the river. Then they were attacked by a large band of Indians. Three of the men in William's party were killed in the attack. When it got dark, the Indians went away. William and the rest of the herders started back towards Kansas. As they were riding along under the moon and the stars, William saw an Indian creeping up on them. He didn't know anything else to do but to shoot the Indian. All the other men congratulated him on such a good shot. But William was very sad. He hadn't wanted to kill anyone. He was just trying to protect himself.

"Now there's a job you should think about, Mary," Grandpa said. "You could herd cattle."

"I don't think I could do that job," Mary laughed.

"Why not? You wouldn't have to worry about being attacked by Indians."

"They usually don't move cows like that anymore, do they? They use trucks and trailers, and I can't drive yet," Mary explained.

"Oh. Well, keep listening. You may hear about something you'd like better."

So anyway, William became famous in Kansas for being such a good shot. Even though his first job herding cattle didn't work out very well, he tried it again. He had to keep working to support his family. It was not hard for him to get work now. Many people knew about him. They all wanted to see the "boy sharp-shooter." He often got jobs as a herder.

Later, he found other kinds of jobs. When he was fourteen, he became a rider for the Pony Express. That was an early way to get mail back and forth between the eastern and the western United States. A couple of years later, he and a friend camped out in central Kansas. They collected beaver skins which a lot of people were wearing as coats or hats.

All this time William was getting better and better at shooting. When he was twenty-one, he became a professional hunter. He had to find enough meat every day to feed 1,100 men who were building a railroad from Kansas to California. He hunted bison, which are often called buffalo. Huge herds of them used to roam freely through the central part of the United States. William became even more famous as a hunter than he had been as a sharp-shooter when he was younger.

Many people thought that William Cody was the best buffalo hunter anywhere. They started calling him Buffalo Bill. However, some people were already calling another man Buffalo Bill. This man's real name was William Comstock. Comstock was also a buffalo hunter. They decided the only way to tell who should be called Buffalo Bill was to have a contest. Everyone agreed that the person who killed the most buffalo in one day would get to be called Buffalo Bill. Early in the morning of the day of the contest, Cody and Comstock rode out to find buffalo. By the end of the day, Comstock had shot forty-six buffalo. But William Cody won. He had shot sixty-nine. William Cody was called Buffalo Bill for the rest of his life.

When he was thirty-six years old, Buffalo Bill finally did what he had always wanted to do. As a boy, he hadn't dreamed about being a famous western hero. He had always wanted to run a circus. But Buffalo Bill's circus was different from the ones you have seen. His circus was about the Wild West. That's what he knew about. He called it Buffalo Bill's Wild West Show. At one time he had hunted Indians. Now he hired them for his show. Acts in his circus included Indians hunting buffalo and cowboys and Indians fighting. Buffalo Bill had some of the most famous Indians and scouts of all time in his show. Sitting Bull and Annie Oakley traveled with it for a while. A favorite part of the show was Buffalo Bill showing how well he could shoot. Balls the size of tennis balls were thrown into the air, and he would shoot them while he galloped around the ring. The show was very popular. He even went to Europe to show them what America's Wild West had been like.

"So you see, dear," Mary's grandfather said, "eleven, or even almost eight, is not too young to get a job. If I were you, I would think about herding cows. I'm sure that would be very exciting."

"Do I really have to get a job?" Mary was beginning to worry now.

"I don't know another way for you to get a bicycle," Grandpa said.

"Well, her birthday is next month," Grandma Elizabeth reminded him.

"That's true," said Grandpa. "She could always ask for a bicycle for her birthday. That would be the easy way."

"Thank you, Grandma. Thank you, Grandpa." Mary kissed them both and ran outside.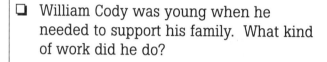

Grandpa George Anderson's Think Box

- ❑ William Cody was young when he needed to support his family. What kind of work did he do?

- ❑ How did William Cody get the name Buffalo Bill?

- ❑ What were some of the things Buffalo Bill did in his circus?

- ○ Work is important. Children of all ages can learn to work, starting at home. What do you do to help your family? Do you also have jobs for which you are paid? Do you save your own money to help your family and others?

Wyatt Earp
Lawman and Friend

B illy was sitting on the porch, dangling
his feet over the edge. With a long stick
he was drawing little circles in the dirt. The
circles were all connected so that they looked
like a chain.

After a while Billy's Uncle Bob closed the book he had been reading. "What have you been thinking about for so long?" he asked. "It's a beautiful day. I thought you would be out playing and upsetting your mother by getting very dirty. No kid that I've known was ever so good at getting dirty as you are. Your father was pretty good at it, though, when we were young."

Billy looked up at his uncle. He had been thinking so hard he had forgotten Uncle Bob was there. "Why are people friends?" he asked with a frown.

"Is this a riddle?" asked Uncle Bob. "People are friends because they like each other."

"Yeah, I know that, but what makes some people like a person, and other people not like the person?"

"Are we talking about any people in particular?" Uncle Bob wanted to know.

"I was thinking about my friend John," Billy said. "He's my best friend, but none of my other friends like him."

"Is that okay with you?" his uncle asked.

"Everybody makes fun of me," Billy said.

"Why do you think the other kids don't like him?" asked Uncle Bob.

"They don't think he's very nice," Billy answered. "Sometimes he wears clothes that they laugh at."

"Are you wondering whether you should keep being friends with him?"

Billy shrugged. "Maybe. I don't like it when they make fun of me."

"But you do still like John," Uncle Bob reminded him.

"Sure."

"Friends are the most important things you can have. No matter what anybody else says, I think you should keep John as your best friend. I know a story about another difficult friendship. Come up here, and I'll tell it to you." Uncle Bob put down his book, and Billy sat in the chair next to him.

This is the story of Wyatt Earp. He was a great lawman of the Wild West. He worked in several of the most dangerous cities of the frontier. He was respected by good and honest people wherever he worked. But he was feared by the bad men and outlaws.

You might think that a man like Wyatt Earp would be friends only with other respected people. A lot of folks thought that he should avoid shady characters. But Wyatt didn't pay much attention to what other people thought. He chose his own friends. He didn't want other people to tell him who to like and who not to like.

Wyatt Earp was born on a farm in Illinois in 1848. He spent more time working on the farm than he did in school. In 1861, his older brothers went to fight in the Civil War. Wyatt was thirteen years old. With his big brothers away, Wyatt had more responsibility to plant and harvest the corn.

In 1864, Mr. Earp decided to take his family west to California. The Earps traveled with several other families in covered wagons. They passed through territory which would become the states of Iowa, Nebraska, Wyoming, and Utah. Along the way, the people in the wagon train had to fight Sioux Indians. Even though it was dangerous, Wyatt loved these frontier areas. In Wyoming he even got a chance to meet Jim Bridger. Jim was a famous trapper and guide who was fond of telling tall tales about his own adventures.

The funny thing about America at that time was that most people lived on the edges of it. Many people lived in the East, of course. That's where America started, and people had been living there for a long time. But when they left the East, many pioneers had gone all the way out to California and Oregon. These settlers had passed through the middle part of the United States without stopping. Very few had stayed to live between the Mississippi River and the Rocky Mountains.

Some people like to live where there aren't many other people around. This is a more difficult and dangerous way to live. It means there aren't folks to help you when things go wrong. It also means there aren't people to keep an eye on you to make sure bad things don't happen to you.

California was already too crowded for Wyatt. He preferred the wide open spaces of the frontier. He knew he could help people in these areas by protecting them from outlaws. He became a lawman so he could do this. One of his first jobs was in Wichita, Kansas. Wichita was called "wild and woolly" because it was so dangerous. Wyatt helped to change that.

In Wichita, Wyatt had to enforce a new law. The law said only lawmen could carry guns in town. The people who made this law hoped it would make Wichita a safer place. But some people, mostly outlaws, were determined to carry their guns in town. They weren't going to let any lawmen tell them what to do.

One day, fifty cowboys rode up to the edge of town. They each wore a gun or two. Their leader, Mannen Clements, had decided to challenge the new law. He didn't think anyone would stand up to his fifty men. One person did stand up to him: Wyatt Earp. Wyatt and nine other deputies were determined to enforce the law. It was ten men against fifty. As Clements' men tried to walk down the street, the deputies stood in their way.

"Mannen, put away your guns," Wyatt Earp ordered. Clements' men didn't move. "Put away your guns, and go back to your camp," Wyatt repeated.

Nobody knows quite why, but that's just what Mannen Clements did. He told all of his men to put away their guns. Then, he led them back to camp. Wyatt Earp became famous for being so brave and standing up to so many people.

Later, he was a lawman in Dodge City, Kansas, and in Tucson and Tombstone which are both in Arizona. All of these towns were dangerous places to live.

Along the way, he met an outlaw dentist named Doc Holiday. They became good friends. Not many people liked Dr. Holiday. This was partly because he was said to have a violent temper. Some people said he was a murderer. Other people called him a thief. All of these people were right, but most people didn't like Doc because he was sick. That's not a good reason not to like someone. Doc had tuberculosis, a disease of the lungs. It made Doc cough a lot. Many people got tuberculosis at that time. Few people get it today because now we know the cure for it. At the time when Doc Holiday had it, many people were scared of it. People were afraid of catching it from him. When there wasn't a cure for tuberculosis, it killed people.

You might wonder why a lawman like Wyatt Earp would be friends with an outlaw with a dangerous disease. Many people wondered just that. Friendship can be a mysterious thing. Often friends don't know just why they like each other. Doc may have liked Wyatt because Wyatt didn't seem to mind that he was sick. So many people seemed to dislike him just because he had a serious illness. Wyatt might have liked Doc because Doc was willing to put himself in dangerous situations to help him. After Doc and Wyatt had become friends, Doc helped Wyatt capture outlaws. Maybe Doc and Wyatt got along so well together because they had something in common. Doc's best friend was Morgan Earp, Wyatt's little brother.

"I don't think that would be very important," Billy said. "I don't like Mary's friends just because she's my sister."

"Like I said," repeated Uncle Bob, "friendship is a mysterious thing. Sometimes it can work that way. You can start to like someone just because he likes someone else that you like."

"Friendship isn't just mysterious," said Billy. "It's confusing."

There was one dangerous mission for which Wyatt didn't have to ask for Doc's help. In fact, he probably couldn't have kept Doc away. That was because it was about Morgan.

It started when Wyatt was in Tombstone, Arizona. Tombstone was a dangerous town.

You could probably guess that just from the name. Wyatt was the marshal of Tombstone, and two of his brothers, Virgil and Morgan, were there to help him.

One night Wyatt and Morgan were playing pool. Two bullets suddenly crashed through the window. One hit the wall just above Wyatt's head. The other one hit Morgan in the back. He didn't live long after that.

Wyatt suspected an outlaw named Curly Bill Brocius. Curly Bill first became a problem for Wyatt when he was still in Kansas. In Arizona, he was still a problem. Not long after the attack at the pool hall, Wyatt caught another outlaw named Indian Charlie. Indian Charlie confessed that he and Curly Bill and two others had planned the attack on the Earp brothers.

Now Wyatt and Doc were determined to find Curly Bill and punish him for killing Morgan. He was able to hide for a while, but not for very long. Wyatt and Doc and a couple of others found Curly Bill hiding in a narrow canyon. Curly Bill and Wyatt shot at each other at almost the same second. Wyatt was the winner.

Not long after they caught Curly Bill, Wyatt and Doc went their separate ways. Nobody, maybe not even they, knew why they had been friends. No one was very surprised when they separated. It's not that they stopped liking each other. Their lives just went in different directions. Wyatt Earp lived to be eighty years old. Despite all the gun fights he was in, he never got hurt. Doc died not long after he and his friend separated. The tuberculosis finally got him.

"Has this story helped you at all with your questions about your friend John?" Uncle Bob asked.

Billy nodded. "I think so. I guess I'll stop asking questions and just like him." 🌿

Uncle Bob Anderson's Think Box

❑ What kind of job did Wyatt have? Did he do his best to keep the town safe?

❑ Who was Wyatt Earp's friend and how did he help?

❑ Why didn't people like Doc Holiday?

○ How can you be a true friend? Everyone needs friends. Can you find a lonely person and be a good friend to him or her?

Alexander Graham Bell

Sound Traveler

Mary woke up very early because it was summer. The early morning sunshine came through her windows and lightly touched her cheek. Sometimes her mother would awaken her like that—with a soft kiss on the cheek. Today, though, the sun was up even before Mary's mother.

Mary liked summertime. She liked the way the sun got up early and stayed up very late. Often it was still up when she went to bed. Mary liked the sounds of summer, too. There were so many sounds, even as early as this. Mary was disappointed, though. She couldn't hear the summer sounds very well up here in her room. She decided to go out on the porch so she could listen better.

Mary knew that it would get very hot later. Right now, though, it would still be cool outside. She dressed quickly and went downstairs. As quietly as she could, she went out on the porch. Then she sat in her favorite chair, closed her eyes, and just listened to all of the summer sounds.

Mary heard many different kinds of birds calling to each other from tree to tree. She also heard birds flying around. She didn't see them because she kept her eyes closed. Mary heard funny bugs chirping in the trees. She remembered that her mother had called them June bugs. Mary heard a few cars drive by. She heard a dog barking far away. She tried to keep track of how many things she could hear, but she lost count somewhere after twenty-five.

Soon after she had given up counting, she heard another sound. Someone was coming through the house toward the porch. Mary tried to decide who it was just from the sounds.

It wasn't Daddy because the steps weren't heavy enough. It wasn't Billy because he always ran. It must be Mommy.

The screen door opened and that someone came out onto the porch. Without opening her eyes, Mary said, "Good morning, Mommy."

"Good morning, dear. How did you know it was me?"

"I just listened," Mary said proudly. "I've been sitting here practicing."

"Well, you're getting very good." her mother said. "Now, if you could just hear me when I call you in for dinner."

Mary laughed. "Oh, Mommy." Then she went on more seriously. "I've been thinking."

"Listening and thinking both in the same day," Mommy said. "I am impressed!"

Mary ignored her mother's joke. "It wouldn't be much fun not be to able to hear things. There are so many things to hear."

Just then they heard a sound inside the house. Mother opened the screen door. "Like the telephone. I'll be right back."

While her mother was talking on the phone, Mary continued listening. When Mommy came back, she said, "That was your Aunt Anne. She wanted to remind us that we are going to her house for lunch today. While I was on the phone, I remembered a story about hearing and telephones. Would you like to hear it?"

"Yes, please," said Mary. "I can practice listening while you tell it." She closed her eyes again and sat very still so she could hear everything her mother said.

This is the story of Alexander Graham Bell. He is the person who invented the telephone. Alexander was born in 1847 in Scotland. For many generations the Bells had taught speech. Alexander's father taught people who were deaf how to speak. He also taught them how to understand people who spoke to them by reading their lips. When he grew up, Alexander would teach these same skills.

While he was in college, Alexander studied acoustics, which is the science of sound. He also did a little work with electricity. Later, he would combine these two things in his famous invention.

In 1868, Alexander's father came to the United States to give some lectures. He spoke about his methods for teaching deaf children to speak. He liked America so much that two years later he moved his whole family here. While his father gave lectures, Alexander set up a school to teach the deaf. He taught them in the same way his father had in Scotland.

Alexander became famous as a teacher. His students did very well. One day he had a very famous visitor. Dom Pedro, the Emperor of Brazil, came to one of Alexander's classes. He wasn't deaf. He just wanted to see the way Alexander could teach.

At that time work was being done with the telegraph. Samuel Morse had invented the telegraph. With it, two people could only talk with short and long clicks. These clicks stood for letters of the alphabet. The system of clicks was called Morse Code.

Alexander wanted to make the telegraph better. He wanted to find a way for people to really talk to each other over long distances. That was when he put together two things that he knew about: sound and electricity. With the help of Thomas Watson, he invented the telephone in 1876.

Telephone is a word that is made up of two Greek words. Tele means "far away" and phone means "sound." The telephone is a machine that brings sound from far away.

At first, no one understood the importance of Alexander Graham Bell's invention. People did not pay any attention to it. He wanted to find a way to show off his invention in public. Not long after he finished the telephone, the Philadelphia Centennial Exposition opened. This was a celebration of the 100th birthday of the United States. Part of the Exposition included the judging of inventions. Alexander felt sure his invention would win once people saw how well it worked.

Late one afternoon, the judges came to see Alexander's telephone. They were grumpy and tired. The judges couldn't see that his invention had any use. They thought it was silly, and they were about to leave without even trying it. Then something surprising happened. Dom Pedro, the Emperor of Brazil, walked by the telephone exhibit. He recognized Alexander as the teacher who had so impressed him years ago. Dom Pedro became excited about the telephone. Soon, he and the judges were all using it. The judges were impressed with Dom Pedro and with Alexander's invention. Soon after the Exposition, everyone knew about the telephone. Everyone wanted to have one.

"And that's the way it still is. Almost everyone has a telephone. Most people can't imagine how they would get along without one," Mary's mother said.

"It sure would be hard without one," Mary said. "You'd have to write letters or go see people all the time."

Mom nodded. "That's right. Without the phone, we might have forgotten to have lunch with your Aunt Anne. You can find out if her neighborhood sounds are different from ours. But that's later. For now, why don't you come inside and practice listening to me make breakfast? You can guess what we're having just from the sounds."

"I don't just want to hear breakfast," Mary said. "I want to taste it. I'm hungry. Listening is hard work."

"I think you're right, dear," her mother agreed. "It must be very difficult. So many people don't do it very well." They went inside laughing. ❧

Katherine Anderson's Think Box

❑ Alexander became a good teacher. What kind of students did he teach?

❑ He wanted to find a way for people to talk over long distances. What does the word "telephone" mean?

❑ What did the judges first think about this new invention? What made them change their minds?

❍ What things would you have to do differently if there were no telephones?

George Armstrong Custer
The Last Stand of Yellow Hair

Billy came running around the corner of
the house. Tommy, his friend from next
door, was right behind him. Billy made a sound
like a bugle when he saw Mary and Tommy's
little brother, Scott. The two younger children
were hiding behind the big oak tree in the front

yard. Tommy yelled, "Charge!" and the two older boys ran to surround the tree.

"Hey, what's all this ruckus?" a voice asked.

All the children stopped and looked around. It took them a little while to figure out where the voice had come from and whose it was. It was Grandpa George. He was sitting in the deep shadows on the front porch.

"We're playing cowboys and Indians," Billy said.

Grandpa smiled. "That sounds like a fun game. Who's who?"

"Scott and I are the Indians this time," Mary answered.

Then Tommy had an idea. "Mr. Anderson, you're old. Did you ever know any real cowboys and Indians?" The children looked at Grandpa George eagerly.

"Well, I may be old, but I'm not that old," he laughed. "I wasn't around when the cowboys and the Indians were still fighting."

Tommy was a little disappointed that Mr. Anderson wasn't old enough. "Do you know any stories about real cowboys and Indians?"

Billy knew the answer to that question before his grandfather said anything. Everybody in his family seemed to know stories about almost everything.

Before he answered Tommy's question, Grandpa George leaned back in his chair, rubbed his chin, and looked up at the sky. "As a matter of fact," he said, "I do know a couple of stories from that time. They aren't happy stories, though. Are you sure you want to hear them?"

The children all said they were sure. "Then sit down around me here, and I'll tell them to you," Grandpa said.

This is the story of the last battle of George Armstrong Custer. Even when he was a boy, Custer wanted to be a great soldier. He went to school at West Point to learn how to be an officer in the United States Army, but he did very badly there. In fact, he did worse than any other student who graduated the same year he did. That might have been the end of his chance for a military career except that the country was fighting a war at that time. He graduated in the middle of the American Civil War. The army needed all of the officers it could get. Custer joined the army and fought for President Abraham Lincoln. He fought in the Union army against the southern Confederate states. He was in many famous battles. Custer even fought at Gettysburg.

A strange thing happened to Custer in the army. Despite doing so badly in military school, he became a great leader. He always seemed to win. No matter how dangerous the mission or how bad things looked for him, he came through.

"Have you heard the latest news about Custer?" people would ask. "He just never seems to lose. I declare, I wish I had just a little piece of that Custer Luck."

After the war was over, the army sent Custer out West to help fight against the Indians.

Mary perked up and poked Scott in the ribs. "Finally, we're getting to the Indian part of the story." She had been thinking that this story was only going to be about cowboys.

"That's right," said Grandpa George, smiling at her. "It's time to talk about the Indians."

The Plains Indians were on the warpath. They had signed a treaty with the United States government. The treaty said that the Indians could have the Black Hills of South Dakota for themselves forever. The Black Hills were sacred to the Indians because many of their people had been buried there. Then gold was found in that area. Miners came in and forced the Indians to leave. The miners didn't care about the treaty. When the Indians tried to defend their land, they were called savages. The army was sent in to keep them from fighting the miners.

The Indians asked a great Sioux chief, Sitting Bull, to lead them. They felt they couldn't lose if he led them. Sitting Bull called a very large number of Indian tribes together.

"I know many of us have been enemies in the past," Sitting Bull said. "But this is more important than our arguments with each other. We must all fight together against the miners and the government of the United States. Only this way will we regain our lands in the Black Hills. These lands were promised to us, and we should be allowed to keep them."

In the summer of 1876, Custer was riding through the Montana Territory. He had been sent to find this large group of Indians. Custer had about 600 soldiers with him. At a creek called Rosebud, he found traces of a large Indian camp. The camp had been about five miles long and three miles wide. Thousands of Indians had been there but had recently moved on. Custer knew that this was the group the army was looking for.

"I'm going to divide my troops," Custer said to his aides. "Major Reno, you and Captain Benteen will lead one group. I will lead the other group. That way we can trap the Indians between us. I hope to catch them at the creek called Little Bighorn."

The group that was led by Major Reno and Captain Benteen were surprised by a large group of Indian braves. Luckily, the soldiers were able to retreat to a hilltop that was covered with boulders. They were able to hold out there until more soldiers came and rescued them. Colonel Custer and his group of soldiers were not so lucky.

When Custer and his men came into the valley of the Little Bighorn, they were attacked by an even larger group of Indian warriors. This group of Indians was led by another chief of the Sioux Indians called Crazy Horse. Crazy Horse's braves quickly surrounded Custer and his troops. The Indians killed every one of the soldiers. That's why this battle is called Custer's Last Stand.

Now, there's one more thing to tell about Custer's loss at the Little Bighorn. Ever since he had graduated from the military academy, Custer had worn his blonde hair long. The Indians called him Yellow Hair. A few days before the Battle of the Little Bighorn, he had his hair cut short. He did it to please his wife.

"Please, dear," she had said, "cut your hair for me. You would look so much more handsome."

After his loss to Sitting Bull and Crazy Horse, people compared him to Samson from the Bible. All of Samson's strength had been in his hair. When he cut it off, he lost his strength.

"Just like Samson," people would say. "All of that Custer Luck must have been in his long blonde hair. As soon as he cut it, he lost a battle."

"But what happened to Sitting Bull and Crazy Horse?" Mary asked. "You didn't tell us much about the Indians."

"That's another story, and I'll have to tell it on another day," Grandpa George replied. "It's almost dinner time. You go wash your hands and get cleaned up. If you want to hear what happened to the Indians after Custer was beaten, I'll meet you here tomorrow at the same time."

"We'll be here!" the children promised as they rushed inside for dinner. ❧

Tommy's Think Box

❑ What promise to the Indians was broken when gold was found in the Black Hills?

❑ What happened to Colonel Custer and his soldiers at Little Bighorn?

○ The greedy miners did not care about the treaty, although it was a promise to the Indians. Promises should be kept. What do you think about breaking promises?

Sitting Bull
The Sioux Chief's Last Battle

The children couldn't wait to hear Grandpa George's story about the Indians. The time between lunch and when they would meet him on the porch went very slowly.

Billy and Tommy spent the afternoon talking about how they would have fought Crazy Horse and his braves. The boys were sure they could have beaten him if they had been at the Little Bighorn.

Mary spent her time making an Indian headdress. She cut the feathers and the headband out of construction paper and then glued them together. When the older boys teased her about how they would have won the battle, she ignored them. She was glad the Indians had won. After all, the soldiers had broken their promise. She pretended to be Sitting Bull by sitting under the big oak tree in the front yard. Sitting Bull greeted all of the other Indians as they arrived. They all brought her presents because she was a great chief. She was happy to accept the presents from them.

Finally, Grandpa came out on the porch.

"Are you ready, children?" he asked. They all shouted that they were ready.

"This is an even sadder story than the one I told you yesterday," he said. "Are you sure you want to hear it?" More quietly this time the children said they wanted to hear the story. "You all remember the story I told you yesterday, I hope," Grandpa said.

The Plains Indians came together in a large group. That group included the tribes of the Sioux, the Cheyenne, the Arapaho, and the Blackfoot. All of these Indian tribes agreed to follow Sitting Bull, the chief of the Sioux. The Indians were upset that their burial grounds in the Black Hills of South Dakota had been taken. They had been attacking settlers and miners, hoping to drive them out. The U.S. Army was called in to stop the Indians and to protect the settlers. The soldier in charge was Colonel Custer.

"You men know why we are here," Custer said to his men. "We are soldiers. We have a sacred duty to protect the citizens of the United States from the savage Indians. We must strike back at the Indians to make them stop attacking settlers and miners."

He and half of his men were killed by the Indians at the creek called the Little Bighorn. That wasn't the first time that the army had fought against the Indians. It was almost the last time the Indians would do battle. Even though the Indians won that day, their victory didn't change things.

Problems with the Indians go back almost to the time when the first Europeans came to this continent. Indians are now often called Native Americans. That is because they lived in this land long before the first explorers and settlers came.

The Native American way of life was much different from that of the settlers who entered their lands. Most Plains Indians did not farm. They lived by hunting. Some followed the great herds of buffalo and antelope as the animals wandered from place to place. Tribes that fished lived by the rivers to be near their fishing grounds. None of the Indian tribes in this area built large cities or roads or anything like that.

Many settlers felt that it was okay to take the land away from the Indians because they planned to use it more fully. The settlers were not simply going to travel through the land, following the animals. They wanted to make permanent homes. The settlers were farmers and ranchers and miners. They did not understand the Indian's way of life; the Indians could not understand the white men's kind of thinking.

The government of the United States tried to solve the problem of who should be able to live on the land by giving certain pieces of land to the Indians. These pieces were called reservations. However, the government couldn't keep other people from moving onto the reservations and taking the land from the Indians. When the settlers moved in, the Indians would strike back in self-defense. This often led to violence on both sides. Then the army would be called in. That is what happened with George Armstrong Custer.

The Battle of the Little Bighorn, where Colonel Custer lost his life, didn't change anything. Even though the soldiers lost the battle, settlers kept taking lands that had been promised to the Indians. The Indians never came together again in as large a group as had fought Custer. Most Indians realized that they could not win. There were too many settlers. The Indians lost hope and few continued to fight.

After the fight with Custer, Sitting Bull went north to Canada. He was afraid of being arrested by the United States Army. He stayed there for six years. Then he worked with Buffalo Bill Cody. Buffalo Bill put on shows with real cowboys and Indians. His shows were like circuses. Sitting Bull was a big hit in these shows.

All this time, small groups of Indians kept attacking settlers. They were trying to get their lands back. Finally, the government decided to stop these attacks by arresting some of the most famous Indian leaders. Sitting Bull was one of the Indian chiefs the army was sent to arrest. They found him sleeping in his camp one night. It was December of 1890, fourteen years after the Battle of the Little Bighorn.

"Get up, old man," the agents said. "Don't try to fight or we'll kill you."

Sitting Bull saw there were many men there to arrest him. He didn't fight. "I will come with you," the chief said. "Just let me put on my clothes. It is cold outside, and there is snow on the ground."

The agents were eager to get out of the camp. They were afraid that they would be attacked by the other Indians in the camp. "No, there's no time for you to get dressed. Come with us quickly."

The agents led Sitting Bull outside. The rest of the camp had been awakened by the approach of the agents. They were all standing outside Sitting Bull's cabin when the chief was brought outside.

"Look, they are taking our chief away," Sitting Bull's people said.

The agents tried to get to their horses, but shots were fired. After a long gunfight, the agents escaped from the camp, but Sitting Bull had been killed. The Indians never fought again. They agreed to be put onto smaller and smaller reservations. Many Native Americans still live on those reservations today.

"That was a sad story," Mary said.

"Yes, it was. I told you it would be," Grandpa George replied.

After a long silence, Billy turned to Mary and said, "Can I be an Indian, too?"

"Sure," said Mary, "if you don't want to be a cowboy anymore."

"I'd like to be an Indian, too," said Tommy.

"Okay," replied Mary.

"All you Indians had better wash up for dinner," Grandpa said.

Mary, with her chief's headdress on, led the other children inside like a good chief should. 🌾

Mary Anderson's Think Box

❏ Why did the settlers think it was okay to take land away from the Indians?

❏ What did Sitting Bull do while he was in Canada?

❏ How did the soldiers treat Sitting Bull when they found him?

⭘ What lessons can you learn from this sad story?

Thomas Alva Edison
The Wizard of Menlo Park

All afternoon it kept getting hotter and
hotter. One by one, the other children
from the neighborhood went inside. Finally, it
was too hot for even Billy and Tommy, his
friend from next door. They gave up when it

was too hot to run. It looked like a big storm was coming.

When Billy went indoors, he found his whole family in the living room. That was the room with the air conditioner. Billy stood in front of the machine and put his face against the vents.

"Don't stand so close, Billy," his mother said. "You'll catch cold."

Cold air was exactly what Billy wanted to catch, but he sat down on the floor next to Mary. He could still feel the cool breeze from the air conditioner there. Just then he heard the first clap of thunder.

"Oh, good, a storm," said Grandpa George. "Maybe it will clear the air a little."

Mom looked out the window. "Looks like it's going to be a big one. Children, please go and make sure all of the windows are closed." As they hurried out of the room, they heard more thunder.

By the time they returned to the living room, it was much darker. The heavy clouds were blocking out the sun. Grandpa had turned on a light so he could keep reading the newspaper.

Just then there was very bright flash of lightning. Right after the lightning, there was a huge thunder clap that made the windows rattle. The noise made Billy jump and Mary squeal.

"Oh my!" exclaimed Grandma Elizabeth.

"If the storm would keep that up," Grandpa said, "I wouldn't need a light to read my paper."

As if the storm had heard him, there was another bright flash of lightning. This time the thunder and lightning seemed to come at exactly the same time. And the storm didn't just make the windows rattle. Grandpa's light and the air conditioner both went off. Mary squealed again.

"Oh my," Grandma said for a second time.

"I wasn't serious about the light," said Grandpa. Billy giggled.

The room was very dark now except for the flashes of lightning. Mom lit some candles. "Don't worry. We can see, but without electricity we can't cook, so dinner may be a bit late."

"It just gets worse and worse," said Grandpa. "I can remember my grandma telling me what it was like before we had electricity."

"But Benjamin Franklin discovered electricity, Grandpa. I remember you told us a story about him. He lived a long time ago."

"You're right, Billy. Benjamin Franklin did live a long time ago, a long time before my grandmother—more than 100 years before. However, it took people a long time to learn how to use electricity. The person who invented the most ways to use electricity was Thomas Edison. It was only after his work that people really understood what electricity could do for them."

"Can you tell us his story?" Mary asked.

"Sure. My eyes are too old to be able to read with only a candle. Come sit on my lap, and I'll tell you his story."

Thomas Alva Edison was born in 1847 in Milan, Ohio. Like most inventors, he was curious, even when he was quite young. He wanted to know why bowls float and how plants grow and why birds have eggs and a thousand other things. He was so interested in the world around him, he couldn't concentrate on what his teacher was saying. Young Thomas would sit staring out of the window and wondering about things.

When he was seven years old, his teacher sent him home with a note for his parents. In it, the teacher said there was no point in sending Thomas to school. The teacher thought he was too stupid to learn anything.

"Am I really stupid?" Thomas asked in tears.

His mother hugged him. "You are not, Al. Don't think that way."

Thomas' mother knew it wasn't true. She went to the school and told the teacher so. From that time on, she taught Thomas at home. He quickly learned what his mother taught him. It helped that she told him he would never be able to answer all the questions that really interested him unless he learned the basics first. After that, he did very well in reading, writing, and arithmetic.

As you will see, he proved that he wasn't stupid at all.

Becoming a famous inventor isn't always just about inventing things. Many people have invented things and not become famous.

"I can't think of any examples right now," Grandpa said. "Of course, that's because those people aren't famous."

Another important part of becoming a famous inventor is showing people that they need what you have invented. This is called "being a good salesman." Not long after Thomas Edison showed that he was curious enough to become an inventor, he showed that he was a good enough salesman to become a famous one.

When he was twelve years old, a railroad was built between Thomas' hometown and Detroit. Thomas asked the railway company if he could sell newspapers and candy on the train. He didn't want a salary from the railroad; rather, he only wanted the profits from his business. The railroad agreed. Thomas was soon doing so well that he hired other young boys to work with him.

Thomas didn't let his new business get in the way of his curiosity, though. The conductor let him set up a chemistry lab in the baggage car so he could do experiments. He was also interested in electricity and the telegraph. There were telegraph offices all along the route of the train. Thomas spent time in these offices learning how the telegraph worked. He also learned Morse Code.

On another day, one of the conductors was playing too roughly with Thomas. The conductor pulled him up the stairs of the train by his ears. This caused an injury which left Thomas partially deaf for the rest of his life.

One day the train shook so badly that Thomas' chemicals fell over. They caused a fire in the baggage car. Thomas was not allowed to work on the train anymore. He didn't mind having to leave his job on the train. Over the years, he had become more and more interested in the telegraph. Now he went to work as a telegraph operator. He would receive messages from one place and send them on to where they were supposed to go. His first invention made the telegraph work better.

Another machine being used at that time was like the telegraph. It was called a stock-ticker. It brought people news of what was happening on the stock market. Thomas invented some improvements for this machine. One of the men who built and sold stock-tickers was very impressed with these inventions. He offered to buy them from Thomas. With the money he made from these inventions, Thomas Edison set up a large lab in New Jersey. He started working as an inventor full time.

Some bad things did happen to Thomas Edison. One day there was a large fire in his workshop. Many of his inventions burned. However, Thomas didn't give up. He went back to work and rebuilt them. Some of them, he built so they were better than they had been before the fire.

Edison invented hundreds of things. One of his inventions was the light bulb. Menlo Park, New Jersey, where he had his workshop, was the first town to have street lights, thanks to Tom. People came from miles around to see them.

"Unfortunately, he didn't invent any light bulbs that don't need electricity. If he had, we wouldn't be sitting here telling stories by candlelight." The children laughed at Grandpa's joke.

He invented the first phonograph. We call it a record player. He invented the machines that made it possible to make movies. He also invented electric motors and batteries which store electricity. All of his inventions had one thing in common. They all made electricity more useful for people. He invented so many marvelous things, he became known as the "Wizard of Menlo Park."

"You surely are a genius," someone once told him.

"Genius," Thomas Edison replied, "is two percent inspiration and ninety-eight percent perspiration." What he meant was that inventing was mostly about hard work.

"I'll tell you, though, if perspiration is all you need to be an inventor, I must be a great one. I'm sweating so much I feel I'm going to melt. I hope the electricity comes on again soon." Grandpa fanned himself with the newspaper.

By that time, the thunder storm had passed. It was beginning to get lighter again. Just then the lights came back on. The air conditioner began blowing cold air again.

"Ah! Just right," said Grandpa. "I've got an idea for you kids. Why don't you make a list of everything in the house that uses electricity? You'll see how important Thomas Alva Edison was." ❦

Grandpa George Anderson's Think Box

❏ What did his teachers in school think about Thomas Edison? What did his mother think?

❏ What did his mother decide to do? Did he learn well?

❏ Find out more about some of the things Thomas invented.

❍ Have you ever been without electricity for more than a day? What did you miss most? It takes hard work to become an inventor. Would you be willing to work that hard to make something new?

George Washington Carver
Food Scientist

Billy walked into the living room and announced, "I want to be a scientist."

Mary looked up from the book she was reading. "Okay," she said and then went back to her reading.

"Do you know of any experiments I should do?" Billy asked.

"No." Mary didn't look away from her book this time.

Billy sat down on the couch next to his sister and sighed loudly. "I have to do some experiments. That's what scientists do."

Mary looked up from her book again. "So do some experiments. Just do them quietly. I'm trying to read."

"But we don't have a chemistry set or anything," Billy complained. "Are there any experiments I can do with things around the house?"

"I don't know." Mary was getting annoyed. Then she had an idea. "Why don't you ask Mommy or Daddy. They would know." She hoped her brother would go into a different room and bother someone else.

"Okay," he said. "I'll go find someone who knows something." As he headed to the kitchen, their father came into the room. Mary sighed. Now she'd never get rid of her brother.

"I want to be a scientist," Billy said. "Are there any experiments I can do just around the house?"

"Of course there are, Son," his father answered. "In fact, we do chemistry every day."

"We do?" Billy was amazed.

"Sure. Every time we cook something, we're doing chemistry," his father said.

Billy was disappointed. "Cooking isn't science."

"Yes, it is," Dad explained. "Part of chemistry is mixing things together and coming up with something completely different."

"Well, maybe." Billy still wasn't sure. "But real scientists don't do stuff like cooking."

"Some scientists do that kind of work," his father said. "It's called food chemistry. There was one great scientist who worked with peanuts and sweet potatoes. Would you like to hear his story?"

"Sure, if he was a real scientist," said Billy. Mary had become interested in what her father was saying. She put down her book so she could listen to the story, too.

This is the story of George Washington Carver. No one is quite sure when he was born. It was some time between 1860 and 1864. That was when Americans were fighting the Civil War.

George was born a slave. The Carvers had a small farm in Missouri. They owned one slave named Mary. She had two children named James and George. One night, slave raiders came to the Carver farm. Slave raiders would steal slaves from one farm and sell them at another. The raiders stole George and his mother. Mr. Carver searched for them the next morning. He found George, who had been left by the side of the road. He never found Mary.

The Carvers were very kind people. They loved George and James and raised them as their own. Mrs. Carver taught the boys to read.

George was a very clever little boy. He loved to read. He wanted to learn about everything, and he was always asking questions. George wanted to go to school to learn more. There wasn't a school anywhere near where the Carvers lived. He had to wait until he was twelve years old. Then he left the Carver farm. The Carvers were sad to see him go.

First, he went to another town in Missouri to go to school. A few years later, he decided to go to a different school. This one was in Kansas. When he arrived there, he found that there was another person named George Carver living in the same town. He decided to change his name to George Washington Carver so that people could tell them apart. He liked the sound of his new name. He liked being named after our first president.

Even when he had finished at the school in Kansas, he still wanted to learn more. George decided to go to college. Very few black people were able to go to college at that time. Finally, he was admitted to Iowa State College. Now he would be able to study what he loved best: plants and farming.

George did very well at college. He graduated in 1896. When he graduated, the president of the college offered him a job. The president wanted him to stay at Iowa State College and teach farming. However, George had received another job offer. This one came from Booker T. Washington, who had started a college called Tuskegee. Tuskegee was a college just for African Americans. Mr. Washington wanted to make sure that African Americans would have a very good college to attend. George couldn't say no to the offer to teach science at Tuskegee.

George Washington Carver started teaching science at Tuskegee College in the fall of 1896. When he got there, he found that he didn't even have a lab in which to teach. That didn't stop him. The first science lesson he taught his students was how to make a lab out of the things they found.

"That's like you, Son," Billy's father said. "The first lesson of science is that you can do it with just about anything."

"But what kind of science were they doing?" asked Billy.

"I think Daddy is just about to tell us," said Mary.

George was very interested in plants and farming. It was farming science, or agriculture, that he taught mostly. At that time, farmers were having a problem in the South. Most farmers grew cotton. Cotton is hard on the soil. After many years of growing cotton on the same piece of land, the soil had gotten tired. The chemicals in the soil that helped cotton grow had been almost used up. George experimented with growing other kinds of plants instead of cotton. One year, he convinced some farmers to plant sweet potatoes. The next year, the farmers grew cowpeas. By the third year, the soil had rested enough to grow cotton again. That year's cotton grew bigger and healthier than it had in a long time. George had solved the problem of tired soil.

Soon, he faced an even bigger problem. Boll weevils were coming into the United States from Mexico. Boll weevils are bugs that eat cotton plants. The farmers were very worried. What could they do about these insects? George thought the answer was easy.

"Plant peanuts instead," he said. "Boll weevils don't like peanuts."

However, George's idea solved only half of the farmers' problem. If they planted peanuts, their crops would be safe from the boll weevils. But who would buy that many peanuts? Farmers make their living by selling their crops. That means they have to grow things that they can sell to people. Up to that time, peanuts had only been used to feed animals. George had to figure out a way to make people want to eat peanuts. George went to work on the problem.

In the end, he came up with 300 ways to use peanuts and 118 ways to use sweet potatoes. After that, many people wanted to buy peanuts and sweet potatoes.

"Can you guess what some of George Washington Carver's inventions were?" their father asked.

"Peanut butter?" asked Billy.

Father nodded. "That's one. Can you think of any others?"

"I can't think of anything else," said Mary.

"George showed that peanuts and sweet potatoes could be used to make face cream, shoe polish, glue, and even ice cream," their father said. "And these are only a few of his ideas."

"I guess there is real science to do in the house," Billy said. 🌿

❑ Why did George change his name when he went to school in Kansas? Why did he like that name?

❑ What subjects did George teach at Tuskegee College?

❑ Cotton is hard on the soil. What experiments did George do to solve that problem?

❑ What other problems did he solve?

○ George Washington Carver was a good problem solver. Can you think of ways to solve problems in your own life and to help others? Do you like to experiment to find better ways to make or do things?

Wilbur & Orville Wright
Flight at Kitty Hawk

"Hey! The sidewalks move by themselves!" Mary exclaimed.

"That's cool!" agreed Billy.

Mary, Billy, and their parents were going on a trip to visit Grandma and Grandpa Williams. The children had not seen their grandparents very often. That was because they lived far away. Their grandparents lived so far away that they were taking a plane ride to visit them.

Everything the children saw in the airport was fun. When they first went into the airport building, they saw a merry-go-round with suitcases and boxes on it. Then, they rode on an escalator like the one at the mall.

They showed their tickets to a woman behind a desk who placed their suitcases on a conveyor belt that carried them away. Billy and Mary each kept their backpacks with books and snacks for the long flight.

Next, they went through the metal detector. When Daddy went through, he made the machine beep because of all the keys he had on his key ring. Now, they were riding on the moving sidewalk down a very long hall. It was so long, they couldn't see the end of it. There were very large windows all along the hall. Billy and Mary could see many planes through the windows. Some were sitting still, and others were moving around. The most exciting ones were taking off and landing. Taking off, a plane went very fast along the ground for a while. Suddenly, its front end and then its back end lifted off the ground. The plane made a lot of noise when it did that.

At last, they reached their gate. There were rows of chairs and another desk there. "This is where our plane will come to pick us up," Mommy said. "When it gets here, we'll go through those big doors with the numbers on them."

"Gate 54," read Mary.

"Airports are really cool," said Billy again.

"You probably don't remember the last time you were in an airport, Billy," his mother said. "You were very young. We were going to my parents' house that time, too."

"I'm sure everybody else on the plane remembers that flight," Billy's father said.

"Why?" asked Mary. "What happened?"

"Let's just say that Billy wasn't very happy to be flying."

"Was I ever at an airport before?" asked Mary.

"No," answered her father. "After our adventure with Billy, we decided we wouldn't try to fly with you children until you were older. I'll go see if our flight is going to be on time."

When Dad came back from the desk, he didn't look happy. "There's fog somewhere. Our flight will be about an hour late."

"Why don't you tell the children a story, dear?" Mom asked. "That will make the time go by more quickly."

"Good idea," said Dad. "I know one about the invention of planes."

"Yeah, good idea," said Billy and Mary together.

The first people to build an engine-powered airplane that would fly were brothers, Wilbur and Orville Wright.

311

"I'm glad you didn't name us Wilbur and Orville," Mary giggled.

"Oh, I don't know," Mom said. "You look more and more like a Wilbur all the time." She leaned over and tickled Mary's tummy. Dad began again.

Wilbur and Orville were the youngest children in a large family. Wilbur was four years older than Orville.

"If Wilbur was born in 1867, Orville must have been born when?"

"Four years later," Billy said. "That would be 1871."

"Very good," Mother said.

You can never tell what is going to inspire an inventor. No one can know ahead of time what will set a person thinking in the right way. For Wilbur and Orville, it was probably a toy helicopter. The boys were about eleven and seven when their parents bought them the toy. They would play with it for hours at a time. The boys would watch the toy very carefully to find out exactly how it worked. When their toy finally broke, they fixed it. From that time, they built many flying machines.

Their parents wanted Wilbur and Orville to have the best education possible. Their father wanted to help them pay for their college education, but he didn't have the money. That was because their mother died when they were still young men. The brothers decided to stay at home to help support the family. They had always been good with mechanical things, so they opened a bicycle shop near their home. When they weren't working on bicycles they built glider airplanes. Those are planes without engines. All they need is wind to fly, like a kite.

All the while, the Wright brothers were planning to build an airplane with an engine. They were using the gliders to study how airplanes fly. Some people in their hometown in Ohio thought they were crazy. Many people didn't think it was possible to build an airplane with an engine that could really fly.

As the Wright brothers worked on the airplane problem, they found they had to test larger and larger gliders. Ohio wasn't a good place to test their large gliders. They needed to find a place where the wind blew strong and steady. They also needed a place with a lot of flat land. They wrote to the United States Weather Bureau asking about such a place. The Weather Bureau told them about Kitty Hawk, North Carolina. The wind always seemed to be blowing there, and it was on the coast so it had long, flat beaches. Kitty Hawk was a perfect place for their tests.

For two years, Wilbur and Orville went to Kitty Hawk every chance they got. By the end of that time, they felt they knew all they needed to know about how planes fly. They were ready for the next step. They were ready to build an airplane with an engine.

When they were sure they were ready, the Wright brothers invited a few people to watch their new plane. On December 17, 1903, Wilbur and Orville first flew their engine-powered airplane in public. It was only in the air for 59 seconds. That's not even a whole minute. Yet it was still something that many people had thought would never happen.

More and more people began to work with and experiment on airplanes. Very soon, they made airplanes better and better: bigger, faster, and able to fly for a much longer time. Now we have thousands of jets flying all over the world every day.

"But even with all of the improvements, airplanes still can't fly very well in the fog. Flights are still late sometimes, and people have to sit around in airports," Dad finished.

"Flight 2116 is now boarding at Gate 54," announced the woman at the ticket desk.

Mom checked their tickets again. "That's our flight."

Billy and Mary had not even seen the plane arrive because they had been listening to their father's story. "Don't forget your backpacks, kids," Dad reminded them. "Next stop, Grandma and Grandpa's house."

"We are sorry for any trouble we have caused you," the woman at the desk apologized as she took their tickets.

"No trouble," said Mary. "We wouldn't have heard the story if the plane had been here on time." ❦

Richard Anderson's Think Box

❑ What toy did their parents give the boys that they liked most? What did they begin building?

❑ To help support the family Wilbur and Orville started a business. What was it?

❑ Did the Wright brothers give up when they were not successful after many tries to make an airplane that would fly?

O Do you know what *patience* means? Did it take lots of patience for Wilbur and Orville Wright to keep working to make a plane that would fly well? Think about that word in your own life. Do you have *patience?*